Mortal Stakes

Also by Robert B. Parker
in Thorndike Large Print ®

Stardust
Playmates
Perchance to Dream
Promised Land
Looking for Rachel Wallace
Early Autumn
A Savage Place
The Widening Gyre

Also by Robert B. Parker
with Raymond Chandler
in Thorndike Large Print

Poodle Springs

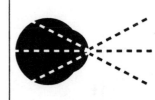

This Large Print Book carries the
Seal of Approval of N.A.V.H.

Mortal Stakes

Robert B. Parker

A Spenser Novel

Thorndike Press • Thorndike, Maine

Library of Congress Cataloging in Publication Data:

Parker, Robert B., 1932-
    Mortal stakes : a Spenser novel / Robert B. Parker.
        p.   cm.
    ISBN 1-56054-314-0 (alk. paper : lg. print)
    1. Large type books. I. Title.
[PS3566.A686M67   1992]   92-23911
813'.54—dc20   CIP

The lines on pages 6, 180 are from "Two Tramps in
Mud Time" from THE POETRY OF ROBERT FROST
edited by Edward Connery Lathem. Copyright 1936 by
Robert Frost. Copyright © 1964 by Lesley Frost
Ballantine. Copyright © 1969 by Holt, Rinehart and
Winston, Inc. Reprinted by permission of Holt, Rinehart
and Winston, Publishers.

Thorndike Large Print® Cloak & Dagger Series edition
published in 1992 by arrangement with Dell
Publishing/Seymour Lawrence, a division of Bantam
Doubleday Dell Publishing Group, Inc.

Cover design by Ron Walotsky.

The tree indicium is a trademark of Thorndike Press.

This book is printed on acid-free, high opacity paper. ∞

*This too is for
Joan, David, and Daniel*

Only where love and need are one,
And the work is play for mortal stakes,
Is the deed ever really done
For Heaven and the future's sakes.

ROBERT FROST

1

It was summertime, and the living was easy for the Red Sox because Marty Rabb was throwing the ball past the New York Yankees in a style to which he'd become accustomed. I was there. In the skyview seats, drinking Miller High Life from a big paper cup, eating peanuts and having a very nice time. I wasn't supposed to be having a nice time. I was supposed to be working. But now and then you can do both.

For serious looking at baseball there are few places better than Fenway Park. The stands are close to the playing field, the fences are a hopeful green, and the young men in their white uniforms are working on real grass, the authentic natural article; under the actual sky in the temperature as it really is. No Tartan Turf. No Astrodome. No air conditioning. Not too many pennants over the years, but no Texans either. Life is adjustment. And I loved the beer.

The best pitcher I ever saw was Sandy Koufax, and the next best was Marty Rabb. Rabb was left-handed like Koufax, but bigger, and he had a hard slider that waited for you to commit yourself before it broke. While I shelled the last peanut in the bag he laid the slider vigorously on Thurman Munson and the Yankees were out in the eighth. While the sides changed I went for another bag of peanuts and another beer.

The skyviews were originally built in 1946, when the Red Sox had won their next-to-last pennant and had to have additional press facilities for the World Series. They were built on the roof of the grandstand between first and third. Since the World Series was not an annual ritual in Boston the press facilities were converted to box seats. You reached them over boardwalks laid on the tar and gravel roof of the grandstand, and there was a booth up there for peanuts, beer, hot dogs, and programs and another for toilet facilities. All connected with boardwalks. Leisurely, no crowds. I got back to my seat just as the Sox were coming to bat and settled back with my feet up on the railing. Late June, sun, warmth, baseball, beer, and peanuts. Ah, wilderness. The only flaw was that the gun on my right hip kept digging into my back. I adjusted.

Looking at a ball game is like looking through a stereopticon. Everything seems heightened. The grass is greener. The uniform whites are brighter than they should be. Maybe it's the containment. The narrowing of focus. On the other hand, maybe it's the tendency to drink six or eight beers in the early innings. Whatever — Alex Montoya, the Red Sox center fielder, hit a home run in the last of the eighth. Rabb fell upon the Yankee hitters in the ninth like a cleaver upon a lamb chop, and the game was over.

It was a Wednesday, and the crowd was moderate. No pushing and trampling. I strolled on down past them under the stands to the lower level. Down there it was dark and littered. A hundred programs rolled and dropped on the floor. The guys in the concession booths were already rolling down the steel curtains that closed them off like a bunch of rolltop desks. There were a lot of fathers and kids going out. And a lot of old guys with short cigars and plowed Irish faces that seemed in no hurry to leave. Peanut shells crunched underfoot.

Out on Jersey Street I turned right. Next door to the park is an office building with an advance sale ticket office behind plate glass and a small door that says BOSTON AMERICAN LEAGUE BASEBALL CLUB. I went in. There was a flight of stairs, dark wood, the walls a pale green latex. At the top another door. Inside a foyer in the same green latex with a dark green carpet and a receptionist with stiff blue hair. I said to the receptionist, "My name is

9

Spenser. To see Harold Erskine." I tried to look like a short-relief prospect just in from Pawtucket. I don't think I fooled her.

She said, "Do you have an appointment?"

I said, "Yes."

She spoke into the intercom, listened to the answer, and said, "Go in."

Harold Erskine's office was small and plain. There were two green file cabinets side by side in a corner, a yellow deal desk opposite the door, a small conference table, two straight chairs, and a window that looked out on Brookline Ave. Erskine was as unpretentious as his office. He was a small plump man, bald on top. The gray that remained was cut close to his head. His face was round and red-cheeked, his hands pudgy. I'd read somewhere that he'd been a minor-league shortstop and hit .327 one year at Pueblo. That had been a while ago; now he looked like a defrocked Santa.

"Come in, Mr. Spenser, enjoy the game?"

"Yeah, thanks for the pass." I sat in one of the straight chairs.

"My pleasure, Marty's something else, isn't he?"

I nodded. Erskine leaned back in his chair and cleaned the corners of his mouth with the thumb and forefinger of his left hand, drawing them together along his lower lip. "My attorney says I can trust you."

I nodded again. I didn't know his attorney.

Erskine rubbed his lip again. "Can I?"

"Depends on what you want to trust me to do."

"Can you guarantee that what we say will be confidential, no matter what you decide?"

"Yes." Erskine kept working on his lower lip. It looked clean enough to me.

"What did my lawyer tell you when he called?"

"He said you'd like to see me after today's game and there'd be a pass waiting for me at the press entrance on Jersey Street if I wanted to watch the game first."

"What do you charge?"

"A hundred a day and expenses. But I'm running a special this week; at no extra charge I teach you how to wave a blackjack."

Erskine said, "I heard you were a wit." I wasn't sure he believed it.

"Your lawyer tell you that too?" I asked.

"Yes. He discussed you with a state police detective named Healy. I think Healy's sister married my lawyer's wife's brother."

"Well, hell, Erskine. You know all you really can know about me. The only way you can find out if you can trust me is to try it. I'm a licensed private detective. I've never been to jail. And I have an open, honest face.

11

I'm willing to sit here and let you look at me for a while, I owe you for the free ball game, but eventually you'll have to tell me what you want or ask me to leave."

Erskine stared at me some more. His cheeks seemed a little redder, and he was beginning to develop callus tissue on his lower lip. He brought his left hand down flat on the top of the desk. "Okay," he said. "You're right. I got no choice."

"It's nice to be wanted," I said.

"I want you to see if Marty Rabb's got gambling connections."

"Rabb," I said. Snappy comebacks are one of my specialties.

"That's right, Rabb. There's a rumor, no, not even that, a whisper, a faint, pale hint, that Rabb might be shading a game now and then."

"Marty Rabb?" I said. When I've got a good line, I like to stick with it.

"I know. It's hard to believe. I don't believe it, in fact. But it's possible and it's got to be checked. You know what even the rumor of a fix means to baseball."

I nodded. "If you did have Rabb in your teacup, you could make a buck, couldn't you?"

Just hearing me say it made Erskine swallow hard. He leaned forward over the desk.

"That's right," he said. "You can get good odds against the Sox anytime Marty pitches. If you could get that extra percentage by having Rabb on your end of the bet, you could make a lot of money."

"He doesn't lose much," I said. "What was he last year, twenty-five and six?"

"Yeah, but when he does lose, you could make a bundle. And even if he doesn't lose, what if you've got money bet on the biggest inning? Marty could ease up a little at the right time. We don't score much. We're all pitching and defense and speed. Marty wouldn't have to give up many runs to lose, or many runs to make a big inning. If you bet right he wouldn't have to do it very often."

"Okay, I agree, it would be a wise investment for someone to get Rabb's cooperation. But what makes you think someone has?"

"I don't quite know. You hear things that don't mean anything by themselves. You see stuff that doesn't mean anything by itself. You know, Marty grooving one to Reggie Jackson at the wrong time. Could happen to anyone. Cy Young probably did it too. But after a while you get that funny feeling. And I've got it. I'm probably wrong. I got nothing hard. But I have to know. It's not just the club, it's Marty. He's a terrific kid. If other people started to get the funny feeling it would destroy him. He'd be gone and no one would even have to prove it. He wouldn't be able to pitch for the Yokohama Giants."

"Hiring a private cop to investigate him isn't the best way to keep it quiet," I said.

"I know, you've got to work undercover. Even if you proved him innocent the damage would be done."

"There's another question there too. What if he's guilty?"

"If he's guilty I'll hound him out of baseball. The minute people don't trust the integrity of the final score, the whole system goes right down the tube. But I've got to know first, and I'm betting there's nothing to it. I've got to have absolute proof. And it's got to be confidential."

"I've got to talk to people. I've got to be around the club. I can't find out the truth without asking questions and watching."

"I know. We'll have to come up with a story to cover that. I don't suppose you play ball?"

"I was the second leading hitter on the Vine Street Hawks in nineteen forty-six."

"Yeah, you ever stood up at the plate and had someone throw you a major-league curve ball?"

I shook my head.

"I have. Nineteen fifty-two I went to spring training with the Dodgers and Clem Labine threw about ten of them at me the first inter-squad game. It helped get me into the front office. Besides you're too old."

"I didn't think it showed," I said.

"Well, I mean, for a ballplayer, starting out."

"How about a writer?" I said.

"The guys know all the writers."

"Not a sports reporter, a writer. A guy doing a book on baseball — you know, *The Boys of Summer, The Summer Game,* that stuff."

Erskine thought about it. "Not bad," he said. "Not bad. You don't look much like a writer, but hell, what's a writer look like? Right? Why not? I'll take you down, tell them you're doing a book and you're going to be hanging around the club and asking questions. It's perfect. You know anything about writing?"

"I've read some," I said.

"I mean, can you sound like a writer? You look like the bouncer at a health club."

"I can keep from sounding as stupid as I look," I said.

"Yeah, okay, it sounds good to me. I see no problem. But you gotta be, for crissake, discreet. I mean dis-goddamn-creet. Right?"

"I am, as we writers say, the very soul of discretion. I'll need a press pass or whatever credentials you people issue. And it is probably smart if you take me down and introduce me around."

"Yeah, I'll take care of that." He looked at me and started working on his lip again. "This is between you and me," he said. "No one else knows. Not the manager, not the owners, not the players, nobody."

"How about your lawyer?" I asked.

"He is my own lawyer, not the club's. He thinks I wanted you for personal business."

"Okay, when do I meet the team?"

Erskine looked at his watch. "Too late today, half of them are showered and gone. How about tomorrow? We'll go in before the game and I'll introduce you around."

"I'll show up here about noon tomorrow then."

"Yeah," he said. "That'll be good. You got a title for this book you're supposed to be writing?"

"I'm looking for sales appeal," I said. "How about *The Sensuous Baseball*?"

Erskine said he didn't like that title. I went home to think of another one.

2

I got up early the next morning and jogged along the river. There were sparrows and grackles mixed in among the pigeons on the esplanade, and I saw two chickadees in the sandpit of one of the play areas. A couple of rowers were on the river, a girl in jeans tucked into high brown boots was walking two Welsh corgis, and there were some other joggers.

Near the lagoon, past the concert shell, a bum in an old blue sharkskin suit was sleeping on a newspaper, and along Storrow Drive the commuter traffic was just beginning. I was still living at the bottom of Marlborough Street and the run up to the BU footbridge took about ten minutes. I crossed the footbridge over Storrow Drive and went in the side door of the BU gym. I knew a guy in the athletic department and they let me use the weight room. I spent forty-five minutes on the irons and another half hour on the heavy bag. By that time some coeds were passing by on their way to class and I finished up with a big flourish on the speed bag. They didn't seem impressed.

I jogged back downriver with the sun much

warmer now and the dew gone from the grass and the commuter traffic in full cry. I was back in my apartment at five of nine, glistening with sweat, and reeking of good circulation, and throbbing with appetite.

I squeezed some orange juice and drank it, plugged in the coffee, and went for a shower. At quarter past nine I was back in the kitchen again in my red and white terry-cloth robe that Susan Silverman had given me on my last birthday. It had short sleeves and a golf umbrella on the breast pocket and the label said JACK NICKLAUS. Every time I put it on I wanted to yell "Fore."

I drank my first cup of coffee while I made a mushroom omelet with sherry, and my second cup of coffee while I ate the omelet, along with a warm loaf of unleavened Arab bread, and read the morning *Globe*. When I finished, I put the dishes in the dishwasher, made the bed, and got dressed. Gray socks, gray slacks, black loafers, and an eggshell-colored stretch knit shirt with small red hexagons all over it. I clipped my holster on over the belt on my right hip. The blue steel revolver was nicely color-coordinated with the black holster and the gray slacks. It clashed badly when I wore brown. To cover the gun I wore a gray denim jacket with red stitching along the pockets and lapels. I checked myself in the mirror. Adorable. Lucky it wasn't ladies' day. I'd get molested at the park.

The temperature was in the mid-eighties and the sun was bright when I got out onto Marlborough Street. I walked a block over to Commonwealth and strolled up the mall toward Fenway Park. It was still too early for the crowd to start gathering, but the early signs of a game were there. The old guy that sells peanuts from a pushcart was pushing it along toward Kenmore Square, an old canvas over the peanuts. A middle-aged couple had parked a maroon Chevy by a hydrant near Kenmore Square and were setting up to sell balloons from the trunk. The trunk lid was up, an air tank leaned against the rear bumper, and the husband, wearing a blue and red tennis visor, was opening a large cardboard box in the trunk. Near the corner of Brookline Ave, outside the subway kiosk, a young man with shoulder-length blond hair was selling small pennants that said RED SOX in red script against a blue background. I looked at my watch: 11:40. You couldn't see the park from Kenmore Square, but the light standards loomed up over the buildings and you knew it was close. As I turned down Brookline Ave toward the park I felt the old feeling. My father and I used to go this early to watch the teams take infield.

I walked the two blocks down Brookline Ave, turned the corner at Jersey Street, and went up the stairs to Erskine's office. He was in, reading what looked like a legal document, his chair tilted back and one foot on the open bottom drawer. I closed the door.

"You think of a new title for that book yet, Spenser?" he said.

An air conditioner set in one of the side windows was humming.

"How about *Valley of the Bat Boys*?"

"Goddamn it, Spenser, this isn't funny. You gotta have some kind of answer if someone asks you."

"*The Balls of Summer*?"

Erskine took a deep breath, let it out, shook his head, as if there were a horsefly on it, kicked the drawer shut, and stood up. "Never mind," he said. "Let's go."

As we went down the stairs, he handed me a press pass. "Keep it in your wallet," he said. "It'll let you in anywhere."

A blue-capped usher at Gate A said, "How's it going, Harold?" as we went past him. Vendors were starting to set up. A man in a green twill work uniform was unloading cases of beer onto a dolly. We went into the locker room.

My first reaction was disappointment. It looked like most other locker rooms. Open lockers with a shelf at the top, stools in front of them, nameplates above. To the right the training area with whirlpool, rubbing table, medical-looking cabinet with an assortment of tape and liniment behind the glass doors at the top. A man in a white T-shirt and white cotton pants was taping the left ankle of a burly black man who sat on the table in his shorts, smoking a cigar.

The players were dressing. One of them, a squat red-haired kid, was yelling to someone out of sight behind the lockers.

"Hey, Ray, can I be in the pen again today? There's a broad out there gives me a beaver shot every time we're home."

A voice from behind the lockers said, "Were you looking for her in Detroit last week when you dropped that foul?"

"Ah come on, Ray, Bill Dickey used to drop them once in a while. I seen you drop one once when I was a little kid and you was my idol."

A tall, lean man came around the lockers with his hands in his back pockets. He was maybe forty-five, with black hair cut short and parted on the left. There were no sideburns, and you knew he went to a barber who did most of his work with the electric clippers. His face was dark-tanned, and a sprinkle of gray showed in his hair. He wore no sweat shirt under his uniform blouse, and the veins were prominent in his arms. Erskine gestured him toward us. "Ray," he said, "I want you to meet Mr. Spenser. Spenser, Ray Farrell, the manager." We shook hands. "Spenser's a writer, doing a book on baseball, and I've arranged for him to be around the club for a while, interview some players, that sort of thing."

Farrell nodded. "What's the name of the book, Spenser?" he said.

"*The Summer Season,*" I said. Erskine looked relieved.

"That's nice." Farrell turned toward the locker room. "Okay, listen up. This guy's name is Spenser. He's writing a book and he'll be around talking with you and probably taking some notes. I want everyone to cooperate." He turned back toward me. "Nice meeting you, Spenser. You want me to have someone introduce you around?"

"No, that's okay, I'll introduce myself as we go," I said.

"Okay, nice meeting you. Anything I can do, feel free." He walked away.

Erskine said, "Well, you're on your own now. Keep in touch," and left me.

The black man on the training table yelled over to the redhead, "Hey, Billy, you better start watching your mouth about beaver. This guy'll be writing you up in a book, and Sally will have your ass when she reads it." His voice was high and squeaky.

"Naw, she wouldn't believe it anyway." The redhead came over and put out his hand. "Billy Carter," he said. "I catch when Fats has got a hangover." He nodded at the black man who had climbed off the table and started toward us. He was short and very wide and the smooth tan coating of fat over his body didn't conceal the thick elastic muscles underneath.

I shook hands with Carter. "Collect all your bubble-gum cards," I said. I turned toward the black man. "You're West, aren't you?"

He nodded. "You seen me play?" he said.

"No," I said, "I remember you from a Brut commercial."

He laughed, a high giggle. "Never without, man, put it on between innings." He did a small Flip Wilson impression and snapped his fingers.

From down the line of lockers a voice said, "Hey, Holly, everybody in the league says you smell like a fairy."

"Not to my face," West squeaked.

Most of the players were dressed and heading out to the field. A short, thin man in a pale blue seersucker suit and dark horn-rimmed glasses came into the locker room. He spotted me and came over. "Spenser?" he said. I nodded. "Jack Little," he said. "I do PR for the Sox. Hal Erskine told me I'd find you here."

I said, "Glad to meet you."

He said, "Anything I can do to help, I'd be delighted. That's my job."

"Do you have biog sheets on the players?" I said.

"You bet. I've got a press book on every player. Stop by my office and I'll have my gal give you the whole packet."

"How old is your gal?" I said.

"Millie? Oh, Christ, I don't know. She's been with the club a long time. I don't ask a lady her age, Spenser. Get in trouble that way. Am I right?"

"Right," I said. "You're right."

"C'mon," he said, "I'll take you out to the dugout, point out some of the players, get you what you might call acclimated, okay?"

I nodded. "Acclimated," I said.

3

I sat in the dugout and watched the players take batting practice. Little sat beside me and chain-smoked Chesterfield Kings.

"That's Montoya," he said. "Alex Montoya was the player of the year at Pawtucket in 'sixty-eight. Hit two ninety-three last year, twenty-five homers."

I nodded. Marty Rabb was shagging in the outfield. Catching fly balls vest-pocket style like Willie Mays and lobbing the ball back to the infield underhanded.

"That's Johnny Tabor. He switch-hits. Look at the size of him, huh? Doesn't look like he could get the bat around. Am I right or wrong?"

"Thin," I said. "Doesn't look like he could get the bat around."

"Well, you know. We pay him for his glove. Strong up the middle, that's what Ray's always said. And Tabor's got the leather. Right?"

"Right."

The crowd was beginning to fill the stands and the noise level rose. The Yankees came out and took infield in their gray road uniforms. Most of them were kids. Long hair under the caps, bubble gum. Much younger than I was. Whatever happened to Johnny Lindell?

Rabb came into the dugout, wearing his warm-up jacket.

"That's Marty Rabb, with the clipboard," Little said. "He pitched yesterday, so today he charts the pitches."

I nodded. "He's a great one," Little said. "Nicest kid you ever want to see. No temperament, you know, no ego. Loves the game. I mean a lot of these kids nowadays are in it for the big buck, you know, but Marty. Nicest kid you ever want to meet. Loves the game."

A man with several chins came out of the alleyway to the clubhouse and stood on the top step of the dugout, looking over the diamond. His fading blond hair was long and very contemporary. It showed the touch of a ten-dollar barber. He was fat, with a sharp, beaked nose jutting from the red dumpling face. A red-checked shirt, the top two buttons open, hung over the mass of his stomach like the flag of his appetite. His slacks were textured navy blue with a wide flare, and he had on shiny white shoes with brass buckles on them.

"Who's that?" I asked Little.

"Don't you know him? Hell, that's Bucky Maynard. Only the best play by play in the business, that's all. Don't let him know you didn't recognize him. Man, he'll crucify you."

"I gather he doesn't work out a lot with the team," I said. Maynard took out a pale green cigar and lit it carefully, turning it as he puffed to get it burning evenly.

"Jesus, don't comment on his weight either," Little said. "He'll eat you alive."

"Is it okay if I clear my throat while he's in the park?"

"You can kid around, but if Bucky Maynard doesn't like you, you got a lot of trouble. I mean, he can destroy you on the air. And he will."

"I thought he worked for the club," I said.

"He does. But he's so popular that we couldn't get rid of him if we wanted. God knows there have been times." Little stopped. His eyes shifted up and down the dugout. I wondered if he was worried about a bug. "Don't get me wrong, now. Buck's a great guy; he's just got a lot of pride, and it don't help to get on the wrong side of him. Course it don't pay to get on the wrong side of anybody. Am I right or wrong?"

"Right as rain," I said. Little liked the phrase. I bet he'd use it within the day. I'm really into language.

Maynard came toward us, and Little stood up. "Hey, Buck, how's it going?"

Maynard looked at Little without speaking. Little swallowed and said, "Like to have you say hello to Mr. Spenser here, doing a book about the Sox."

Maynard nodded at me. "Spenser," he said. His southern accent stretched out the last syllable and dropped the *r*.

"Nice to meet you," I said. I hoped he wasn't offended.

"He'll be wanting to talk to you, Buck, I know. No book about the Sox would be worth much if Old Buck wasn't in it. Am I right, Spenser, or am I right?"

"Right," I said. Little lit a new Chesterfield King from the butt of the old one.

Maynard said, "Why don't y'all come on up the booth later on and watch some of the game? Get a chance to see how a broadcast team works."

"Thanks," I said, "I'd like to."

"Just remember you're not going to get any predigested Pablum up there. In mah booth by God we call the game the way it is played. No press release bullshit; if a guy's doggin' it, by God we say he's doggin' it. You follow?"

"I can follow that okay."

Maynard's eyes narrowed as he looked at me. They were pale and small and flat, like two Necco wafers. "You better believe it 'cause anyone who knows me knows it's true. Isn't that right, Jack?"

Little answered before Maynard finished asking. "Absolutely, Buck, anybody knows that. Bucky tells it like it is, Spenser. That's why the fans love him."

"C'mon up, Spenser, anytime. Jack'll show you the way." Maynard rolled the green cigar about in the center of his mouth, winked, and moved out onto the field toward the Yankee dugout.

Billy Carter from the end of the dugout yelled, "Whale, ho," and then stared out toward the right-field stands as Maynard whirled and looked into the dugout. Ray Farrell had come out of the dressing room and was posting the lineup at the far end of the dugout. He ignored Carter and Maynard. Maynard looked for maybe a minute into the dugout while Carter observed the right-field foul line from under the brim of his cap, his feet cocked up against one of the dugout supports. He was whistling "Turkey in the Straw." Maynard turned and continued toward the Yankee dugout.

Little blew out his breath. "That goddamned Carter is going to get in real trouble someday. Always the wisecracks. Always the goddamned hot dog. He ain't that good. I mean, he catches maybe thirty games a year. You'd think he'd be a little humble, but always the big mouth." Little spilled some ashes onto his shirtfront and brushed them off vigorously.

"I was thinking about some Moby Dick humor myself when Maynard was standing there blotting out the sun."

"You screw around with Bucky and you'll never get your book written, I'll tell you that straight out, Spenser. That's no shit." Little looked as if he was in pain, his small-featured face contorted with sincerity. Farrell went up the steps of the dugout and out toward home plate with his lineup card. The Yankee manager came out toward home plate from the other side, and, for the first time, I saw the umpires. Older than the players, and bulkier.

"I think I'll go up in the broadcast booth," I said. "If Maynard turns on me and truths me to death, I want you to write my mom."

Little didn't even want to talk about it. He brought me up to the press entry, along the catwalk, under the roof toward Maynardville.

The broadcast booth was a warren of cable lash-up, television monitors, microphone cords, and one big color TV camera set up to point at a blank wall to the rear of the booth. For live commercials, I assumed. Give Bucky Maynard a chance to tell it like it is about somebody's bottled beer. There were two men in the booth already. One I recognized. Doc Wilson, who used to play first base for the Minnesota Twins and now did color commentary for the Sox games. He was a tall, angular man, with rimless glasses and short, wavy brown hair. He was sitting at the broadcast table, running through the stat book and drinking black coffee from a paper cup. The other man was young, maybe twenty-two, middle height and willowy with Dutch boy blond hair and an Oakland A's mustache. He had on a white safari hat with a wide leopard-skin band, pilot's sunglasses, a white silk shirt open to the waist, like Herb Jeffries, and white jeans tucked into the top of rust-colored Frye boots. There was a brass-studded rust-colored woven leather belt around his waist and a copper bracelet on his right wrist. He was slouched in a red canvas director's chair with his feet up on the broadcast counter, reading a copy of the *National Star* and chewing gum.

Wilson looked up as we came in. "Hey, Jack, howsa kid?"

"Doc, say hello to Spenser, here. He's a writer, doing a book on the Sox, and Bucky invited him up to the booth for a look-see."

Wilson reached around, and we shook hands. "Good deal," he said. "If Buck says go, it's go. Anything I can help with, just give a holler." The kid in the safari hat never looked up. He licked his thumb, turned a page of the *Star*, his jaws working smoothly, the muscles at the hinge swelling regularly as he chewed.

Little said, "This here's Lester Floyd. Lester, this is Mr. Spenser."

Lester gave a single upward jerk of his head, raised one finger without releasing the magazine, and kept reading. I said, "What's he do, sing 'Flamingo' at the station breaks?"

The kid looked up then. I couldn't see his eyes behind the amber lenses of his aviator shades. He blew a large pink bubble, popped it with his teeth, and slowly chewed it back into his mouth.

Little said, "Lester is Bucky's driver, Spenser. Spenser's going to be doing a book on the Sox and on Bucky, Lester."

Lester blew another big bubble and chewed it back in. "He's gonna be looking up his own asshole if he gets smart with me," he said. There was a red flush on his cheekbones.

"Guess he doesn't sing 'Flamingo,' " I said to Wilson.

"Aw now, Lester, Mr. Spenser's just kidding around." Little did a small nervous shuffle step. Wilson was staring out at the diamond. Lester was working harder on the gum.

32

"And I'm telling him not to," Lester said.

"Never mind, Lester." The voice came from behind me. It was Maynard. "Ah invited Mr. Spenser up here to listen to mah broadcast. He's mah guest."

"He said something smart about me singing, Bucky. I don't like that sorta talk."

"Ah know, Lester, ah don't blame you. Mr. Spenser, ah'd appreciate it if you was to apologize to Lester here. He's a good boy, but he's very emotional. He's also got a black belt in tae kwon do. And ah wouldn't want to get your writing hand all messed up before you even start."

Waltzing with Lester in the broadcast booth wasn't going to tell me anything about Marty Rabb. If he was any good, it might tell me something about me, but that wasn't what I was getting paid for. Besides, I knew about me. And if I was a writer, I wasn't supposed to be roughing it up with black belts. Maybe box with José Torres on a talk show, but brawling at a ball game . . . ? "I'm sorry, Lester," I said. "Sometimes I try too hard to be funny."

Lester popped his gum at me again and went back to the *National Star*. Maynard smiled with his mouth only and moved to a big upholstered swivel chair at the broadcast table. He sat down, put on big padded earphones, and spoke into the mike. The small monitor built into the table to his right had flickered into life and displayed a picture of the batter's box below. There was a long mimeographed list in front of him on a clipboard, and he checked off the first two items as he spoke.

"Burt, ah want to open on Stabile warming up. Doc and me will do some business about the knuckler and how it flutters. Right? . . . Yup, soon's you run the opening cartridge."

Wilson looked over and said to me, "He's talking to the people outside in the truck." I nodded. Lester licked his thumb again and turned another page.

Little leaned over and whispered to me. "Gotta run, anything you need just let me know." I nodded again, and Little tiptoed out like a man leaving church early.

Maynard said to the people in the truck, "Ah got nothing to do live up here, right? . . . well, ah don't see nothing on the sheet . . . no, goddamn it, ah taped that yesterday afternoon . . . okay, well get it straight, boy."

A cartoon picture of a slightly loutish-looking baseball player in a Red Sox uniform appeared on the monitor. Maynard said, "Twenty seconds," to Wilson. Below and to our right along the first-base line a portly right-handed pitcher named Rick Stabile was warming up. He threw without effort, lobbing the ball toward the catcher.

Wilson said into his mike, "Good afternoon, everyone, from Fenway Park in Boston, where today the Red Sox go against the Yankees in the rubber game of a three-game series. This is Doc Wilson along with Bucky Maynard standing by to bring you all the action."

A beer commercial appeared on the monitor screen, and Wilson leaned back. "You gonna pick it up on Stabile, Buck?"

Maynard said, "Check." Wilson handed him the stat sheet and leaned forward as the beer company logo filled the monitor screen. Lester was finished with the tabloid and settled down into his chair and apparently went to sleep. He looked like a peaceful serpent. Tae kwon do? Never tried somebody that did that. I gave him a hard look. He was motionless; the breath from his nostrils ruffled his mustache gently. He was probably paralyzed with fear. Maynard said, "Howdy, all you Red Soxers, this is the old Buckaroo and you're looking at Rick Stabile's butterfly . . ."

By the sixth inning the game was gone for Boston. Stabile's knuckler had apparently deked when it should have dived, and the Yankees led 11 to 1. I made two trips, one for beer and hot dogs and one for peanuts. Lester slept, and Maynard and Wilson tried to talk some excitement into a laugher.

"Stabile's got to get some of the lard off from around his middle, Doc."

"Well, he's a fine boy, Bucky, but he's been playing a little heavy this year."

"Tell it like it is, Doc. He came into spring training hog fat and he hasn't lost it. He's got the tools, but he's gotta learn to back off from the table or he'll eat himself right out of the league." Maynard checked off an item on his log sheet.

"Here's Graig Nettles, two for two today, including the downtowner in the first with Gotham on all the corners."

I got up and headed out of the booth. Wilson winked at me as I left.

I stopped by at Little's office to pick up the press kit on Marty Rabb and four others. Little's gal had dentures.

4

Steam from the showers drifted into the locker room and made the air moist. The final score was 14 to 3 and no one was pouring champagne on anyone. I sat down beside Marty Rabb. He was bent over, unlacing his spikes. When he straightened, I said, "My name's Spenser, I'm writing a book about the Sox, and I guess I oughta start with you."

Rabb smiled and put out his hand. "Hi, glad to help. How about you don't mention today, though, huh?" He shook his head. He was well above my six feet one — all flat planes and sharp angles. His short brown hair grew down over his forehead in a wedge. His head was square and long, like a square-bladed garden spade. His cheekbones were high and prominent, making the cheeks slightly hollow beneath them.

I said, "Bucky Maynard tells me Stabile's too fat and that's why he's having trouble."

"You ever see Lolich or Wilbur Wood?" Rabb said.

"Yeah," I said. "I've seen Maynard too."

Rabb smiled. "Ricky doesn't pitch with his stomach. The ball wasn't moving for him

37

today, that's all."

"It was moving for you yesterday."

"Yeah, I had it grooved yesterday." Rabb undressed as he talked. He was long-muscled and bony, his body pale in contrast to the dark tan on his face, neck, and arms.

"Well," I said, "I'm really more interested in the human side of the game, Marty. Could we get together tonight and talk a little?"

Rabb was naked now, standing with a towel over his shoulder. In fact, most of the people in the dressing room were naked. I felt like a streaker in a nudist colony.

"Yeah, sure. Ah, lemme see, no, we're not doing anything tonight that I know of. Why don't you come over to the apartment, meet my wife, maybe have a drink? That okay with you?"

"Fine, what time?"

"Well, the kid goes to bed about seven — about seven thirty. Wanna do that?"

"Yes. Where?"

"Church Park. You know where that is?"

"Yeah."

"Apartment six twelve."

I looked at my watch: 4:35. "That's fine. I'll be there. Thanks very much."

"See you." Rabb headed for the showers. His body high and narrow, the left trapezius muscle overdeveloped, swelling out along the left side of his spine.

I left. Outside the dressing room there were two people sweeping. Other than that the place was empty. I walked up the ramp under the stands and looked out at the field. It was empty. I went down and hopped the railing of the box seats. There was no sound. I walked over to home plate. The wall in left seemed arm's length away and 300 cubits high. The sun was still bright and at that time of day slanted in over the third-base stands, and the shadows of the light towers looked like giant renderings by Dali. A pigeon flew down from the center-field bleachers and pecked at the warning track. I walked out to the pitcher's mound and stood with my right foot on the rubber, looking down into home plate. Traffic sounds drifted in from the city, but muffled. I put my right hand behind me and let it rest against my butt. Left hand relaxed on my left thigh. I squinted in toward the plate. Last of the ninth, two out, three on, Spenser checks the sign. One of the men who'd been sweeping came out of the passageway and yelled, "Hey, what the hell are you doing out there?"

"Striking out Tommy Henrich, you dumb bastard. Don't you know anything?"

"You ain't supposed to be out there."

"I know," I said. "I never was."

I walked back in through the stands and

on out of the ball park. I looked at my watch. It was nearly five. I walked back down the Commonwealth Avenue mall to Massachusetts Avenue. If Commonwealth Ave is yin, then Mass Ave is yang. Steak houses that no one you knew had gone to, office buildings with dirty windows, fast food, a palm reader, a massage parlor. I crossed Mass Ave and went into the Yorktown Tavern. It had plate glass windows and brown linoleum, a high tin ceiling painted white, booths along the left, a bar along the right. In the back corner was a color TV carrying a bowling game called *Duckpins for Dollars*. No one was watching. All the barstools were taken, and most of the booths. No one was wearing a tie. No one was drinking a Harvey Wallbanger. The house special was a shot and a beer.

In the last booth on the left, alone, was a guy named Seltzer who always reminded me of a seal. He was sleek and plumpish, thin through the chest, thicker through the hips. His hair was shiny black, parted in the middle and slicked tight against his head. He had a thin mustache, a pointed nose, and a dark pinstriped suit that cost at least $300. His white shirt gleamed in contrast to the darkness of the suit and the dinginess of the bar. He was reading the *Herald American*. As I slid in opposite him, he turned the page and folded it neatly back. I could see the big diamond ring on his little finger and the diamond chips set in the massive silver cuff links. He smelled of cologne, and when he looked up at me and smiled, his white teeth were even, cap perfect in his small mouth.

I said, "Evening, Lennie."

He said, "You know, Spenser, little things break your balls. You ever notice that? I mean I used to read the *Record American*, right? Nice little tabloid size, easy to handle. Then they buy up the *Herald* and go the big format and it's like reading a freakin' road map. Now that busts my nuts, trying to fold this thing right. That kinda stuff bother you ever?"

"On slow days," I said.

"Want a drink?"

"Yeah, I'll have a brandy Alexander," I said.

Seltzer laughed. "Hey, Frank." He raised a finger at the bartender. "A shot and a beer, okay?"

The bartender brought them over, put the beer on a little paper coaster, and went back behind the bar. I drank the shot.

"Well," I said, "if I had worms, I guess they're taken care of."

"Yeah, Frank don't age that stuff all that long, does he?"

I sipped the beer. It was better than the

whiskey. "Lennie, I need to know something without letting it get around that I'm asking." His skin was remarkable. Smooth and pale and unlined. The sun had rarely shone upon it. It made him look a lot younger than I knew he was.

"Yeah," he said. "Sure, kid. I never saw any advantage talking about things for no good reason. What do you want to know?" He sipped some beer, holding the glass in the tips of his fingers with the little finger sticking out. When he put the glass down, he took the handkerchief from his breast pocket and wiped his mouth carefully.

"I want to know if you've heard anything about Marty Rabb."

Seltzer was very careful putting the handkerchief back in his pocket. He got the three points arranged and stood half up in the booth to look across the bar into the mirror and make sure they were right.

"Like what?" he said.

"Like anything at all."

"You mean, does he occasionally place a wager? That kind of thing?"

"That, or anything else."

"Well, he never placed a bet with me," Seltzer said, "but I heard something peculiar about him. The odds seem to shift a little when he pitches. I mean, there's some funny money placed when he's scheduled to go. Nothing big, nothing I'd even think about if somebody like you didn't come around and ask about him."

"You think he's in the satchel?"

"Rabb? Hell, no, Spenser. Nothing that strong. There's just a whisper, just a ruffle, that not everything is entirely jake. I wouldn't hesitate taking money when Rabb's pitching. I don't know anyone that would. It's just . . ." He shrugged and spread his hands out palms up. "Want another drink?"

I shook my head. "The last one took the enamel off my front teeth," I said.

"Aw, Spenser." Seltzer shook his head. "You're going soft. I remember twenty years ago you was fighting prelims in the Arena, you thought that stuff was imported from France."

"In those days I don't remember you dressing like George Brent either," I said.

Seltzer nodded. "Yeah," he said, "things change. Now instead of a newspaper, they give you a freakin' road map. You know?"

I left him refolding his paper and went to get something to eat. The bar whiskey was thrashing about in my stomach, and I thought maybe I could smother it with something.

5

I had two cheeseburgers and a chocolate shake at an antique brick McDonald's on Huntington, just down from Symphony Hall. The food throttled the whiskey okay, but I was furtive coming out. If anyone saw me, I could never eat at Locke-Ober's again. The guilty part was I liked the cheeseburgers.

It was a little after six and I had some time to kill. There seemed to be more of it and harder to kill as I got older. I strolled back down Mass Ave toward the river. The college kids were out on the esplanade in large numbers, and the air was colorful with Frisbees and sweet with the smell of grass. I sat on a bench near the Mass Ave Bridge and looked at the river and watched a boy and girl share a bottle of Ripple. Sailboats veered and drifted on the river, and an occasional powerboat left a rolling wake upstream. Across the river MIT loomed like a concrete temple to the Great God Brown. A six-foot black girl with red hot pants and platform sandals went by with a Lhasa apso on a short leash. I watched her out of sight around the bend westbound.

At seven fifteen I strolled back up Mass Ave

toward Church Park. Church Park is a large, gray, cement urban development associated with the Christian Science church complex across the street. It replaced a large number of shabby brick buildings with a very long twelve-story cement one that had stores on the bottom floor and apartments above. The doorman made me wait while he called up.

When I came out of the elevator, Marty Rabb was at his door, looking down the corridor at me. There was something surrealistic about the way his head appeared to violate the fearful symmetry of the hall.

"Down this way, Spenser," he said. "Glad to see you."

The front door opened into the living room. To the right a bedroom, straight ahead a small kitchen. To the left the living room opened out toward the street and looked out at the dome of the Mother Church of Christ Scientist across the street. Traffic sound drifted up through the open windows. The living room was done in wall-to-wall beige carpet; the walls were egg-shell white. There were framed mementos of Rabb's career scattered on the walls. The furniture was in browns and beiges, and the tone was modern. On the glass-topped coffee table near the couch were a tray of raw vegetables and a bowl of sour cream dip.

"Honey, this is Mr. Spenser that's writing the book," Rabb said. "Spenser, this is my wife, Linda."

We shook hands. She was small and black-haired. Her features were small and close together, and her eyes dominated her face. They were very round and dark, with long lashes. Her black hair was long down her back and pulled back at the nape of her neck with a dark wooden clip. She had on a salmon pink sleeveless shell and white jeans. Her makeup was so understated that at first I thought she wore none.

"Nice to meet you, Mr. Spenser. Why don't you have a seat here on the couch? It's closest to the dip." She smiled, and her teeth were small and rather sharp.

I said, "Thank you."

"Would you like a hard drink, Mr. Spenser, or beer?" Rabb said. "I got some nice ale from Canada, Labatt Fifty, you ever try it?"

"Tried and approved," I said. "I'll take the ale."

"Honey?"

"You know what I'd love, that we haven't had in a while, a Margarita. Have we got the stuff to make a Margarita, Marty?"

"Yeah, sure. We got about everything."

"Okay, and put a lot of salt on the rim," she said.

She sat on one of the big armchairs opposite the couch, kicked her sandals off, and tucked her feet up under her. "Tell me about this book you're writing, Mr. Spenser."

"Well, Mrs. Rabb —"

"Linda."

"Okay, Linda. I suppose you'd say it's along the lines of several others, looking at baseball as the institutionalized expression of human personality." She nodded and I wondered why. I didn't know what the hell I'd just said.

"Isn't that interesting," she said.

"I like to see sports as a kind of metaphor for human life, contained by rules, patterned by tradition." I was hot now, and rolling. Rabb came back with the Margarita in a low-ball glass and the ale in Tiffany-designed goblets that said COCA-COLA. I thought Linda Rabb looked relieved. Maybe I wouldn't switch to the talk show circuit yet. Rabb passed out the drinks.

"What's patterned by tradition, Mr. Spenser?" he said.

"Sports. It's a way of imposing order on disorder."

Rabb nodded. "Yeah, right, that's certainly true," he said. He didn't know what the hell I had just said either. He drank some of the ale and put some dry-roasted cashews in his

47

mouth, holding a handful and popping them in serially.

"But I'm here to talk about you, Marty, and Linda too. What is your feeling about the game?"

Rabb said, "I love it," at the same time that Linda said, "Marty loves it." They laughed.

"I'd play it for nothing," Rabb said. "Since I could walk, I been playing, and I want to do it all my life."

"Why?" I said.

"I don't know," Rabb said. "I never gave it any thought. When I was about five my father bought me a Frankie Gustine autograph glove. I can still remember it. It was too big for me and he had to buy me one of those little cheap ones made in Taiwan, you know, with a couple of little laces for webbing? And I used to oil that damn Frankie Gustine glove and bang my fist in the pocket and rub some more oil until I was about ten and I was big enough to play with it. I still got it somewhere."

"Play other sports?" I didn't know where I was going, but I was used to that.

"Oh yeah, matter of fact, I went to college on a basketball scholarship. Got drafted by the Lakers in the fifth round, but I never thought about doing anything else but baseball when I got out."

"Did you meet Linda in college?"

"No."

"How about you, Linda, how do you feel about baseball?"

"I never cared about it till I met Marty. I don't like the traveling part of it. Marty's away about eighty games a season. But other than that I think it's fine. Marty loves it. It makes him happy."

"Where'd you two meet?" I asked.

"It's there in the biog sheet, isn't it?" Rabb said.

"Yeah, I suppose so. But we both know about PR material."

Rabb said, "Yeah."

"Well, let's do this. Let's run through the press kit and maybe elaborate a little." Linda Rabb nodded.

Rabb said, "It's all in there."

"You were born in Lafayette, Indiana, in nineteen forty-four." Rabb nodded. "Went to Marquette, graduated nineteen sixty-five. Signed with the Sox that year, pitched a year in Charleston and a year at Pawtucket. Came up in nineteen sixty-eight. Been here ever since."

Rabb said, "That's about it."

I said, "Where'd you meet Linda?"

"Chicago," Rabb said. "At a White Sox game. She asked for my autograph, and I said, yeah, but she had to go out with me. She did. And bingo."

I look at my biog sheet. "That would have been in nineteen seventy?"

"Right." My glass was empty, and Rabb got up to refill it. I noticed his was less than half gone.

"We were married about six months later in Chicago." Linda Rabb smiled. "In the off-season."

"Best thing I ever did," Rabb said, and gave me a new bottle of ale. I poured it into the glass, ate some peanuts, and drank some ale.

"You from Chicago, Linda?"

"No, Arlington Heights, a little bit away from Chicago."

"What was your maiden name?"

Rabb said, "Oh for crissake, Spenser, why do you want to know that?"

"I don't know," I said. "You ever see one of those machines that grades apples, or oranges, or eggs, that sort of thing, by size? They dump all sizes in the hopper and the machine lets the various sizes drop into the right holes as it works down. That's how I am. I just ask questions and let it all go into the hopper and then sort it out later."

"Well, you're not sorting eggs now, for crissake."

"Oh, Marty, let him do his job. My maiden

name was Hawkins, Mr. Spenser."

"Okay, Marty, let's go back to why you love baseball," I said. "I mean, think about it a little. Isn't it a game for kids? I mean, who finally cares whether a team beats another team?" It sounded like the kind of thing a writer would ask, and I wanted to get them talking. Much of what I do depends on knowing who I'm doing it with.

"Oh, Christ, I don't know, Spenser. I mean, what isn't a game for kids, you know? How about writing stories, is that something for grown-ups? It's something to do. I'm good at it, I like it, and I know the rules. You're one of twenty-five guys all working for something bigger than they are, and at the end of the year you know whether or not you got it. If you didn't get it, then you can start over next year. If you did, then you got a chance to do it again. Some old-timey ballplayer said something about you have to have a lot of little boy in you to play this game, but you gotta be a man too."

"Roy Campanella," I said.

"Yeah, right, Campanella. Anyway, it's a nice clean kind of work. You're important to a lot of kids. You got a chance to influence kids' lives maybe, by being an example to them. It's a lot better than selling cigarettes or making napalm. It's what I do, you know?"

"What about when you get too old?"

"Maybe I can coach. I'd be a good pitching coach. Maybe manage. Maybe do color. I'll stay around the game one way or another."

"What if you can't?"

"I'll still have Linda and the boy."

"And when the boy grows up?"

"I'll still have Linda."

I was getting caught up in the part. I'd started to lose track. I was interested. Maybe some of the questions were about me.

"Maybe I better finish up my Labatt Fifty and go home," I said. "I've taken enough of your time."

Linda Rabb said, "Oh no, don't go yet. Marty, get him another beer. We were just getting started."

I shook my head, drained my glass, and stood up. "No, thank you very much, Linda. We'll talk again."

"Marty, make him stay."

"Linda, for crissake, if he wants to go, let him go. She does this every time we have company, Spenser."

They both walked with me to the door. I left them standing together. He towered over her in the doorway. His right arm was around her shoulder, and she rested her left hand on it. I took a cab home and went to bed. I was working my way through Samuel

Eliot Morison's *The Oxford History of the American People,* and I spent two hours on it before I went to sleep.

6

It was dead quiet in my bedroom when I woke up in the morning. The sun vibrated in the room and the hum of my air conditioner underlined the silence. I lay on my back with my hands behind my head for a while and thought about what was bothering me about Linda Rabb.

What was bothering me was that she'd said she knew nothing about baseball till she met Marty but that she'd met Marty at a ball game when she'd asked for his autograph. The two didn't go together. Nothing much, but it didn't fit. It was the only thing that didn't. The rest was whole cloth. Middle American jock-ethic-kid and his loving wife. In the off-season I bet he hunted and fished and took his little boy sliding. Would he be going into the tank? "It's what I do," he'd said. "I know the rules." I could understand that. I knew about the need for rules. I didn't believe he'd dump one. I never believed Nixon would be President either. I got up, did 100 push-ups, 100 sit-ups, took a shower, got dressed, and made the bed.

There's a restaurant in Portsmouth, New

Hampshire, which makes whipped cream biscuits, and I got the recipe once while I was up there having dinner with Brenda Loring. I made some while the coffee perked, and while they baked I squeezed a pint of orange juice and drank it. I had the biscuits with fresh strawberries and sour cream and three cups of coffee.

It was nearly ten o'clock when I got out onto the street. There was a bright smell of summer outside my apartment house. Across Arlington Street the Public Garden was a sunny pleasure. I strolled on past the enormous Thomas Ball statue of Washington on horseback. The flower beds were rich with petunias and redolent of pansies against a flourish of scarlet snapdragons. The swan boats had begun to cruise the pond, pedaled by college kids in yachting caps and trailed by an orderly assemblage of hungry ducks that broke formation to dart at the peanuts the tourists threw. I crossed the bridge over the swan boat lake and headed toward the Common on the other side of Charles Street. At the crossing there was a guy selling popcorn from a pushcart and another selling ice cream and another selling balloons and little monkeys dangling from thin sticks and blue pennants that said BOSTON, MASS., in yellow script. I turned right, walked up Charles toward

Boylston. At the corner was the old guy that takes candids with a big tripod camera; faded tan samples were displayed in a case on the tripod. I turned up Boylston toward Tremont and down Tremont toward Stuart. My office was on Stuart Street. It wasn't much of an office, but it suited the location. It would have been an ideal spot for a VD clinic or a public exterminator.

I opened the window as soon as I got in. I'd have to remember not to do push-ups on the days I had to open that window. I hung up my blue blazer, sat down at my desk, got my yellow pad out, and pulled the phone over. By one thirty I had pretty well confirmed Marty Rabb's biography as stated. The town clerk's office in Lafayette, Indiana, established that Marty Rabb had in fact lived there and that his parents still did. The office of the registrar at Marquette confirmed his attendance and graduation in 1965. I called a cop I knew in Providence and asked him if they had anything on Rabb when he was at Pawtucket. He called me back in forty minutes to say no. He promised me he'd keep his mouth shut about my question, and I half thought he would. He was as trustworthy as I was likely to find.

Linda Rabb was more of a problem. There was no record of her marriage to Rabb at the

Chicago Hall of Records. As far as they knew, Marty Rabb hadn't married Linda Hawkins or anyone else in Chicago in 1970 or any other time. Maybe they got married by some JP in a suburb. I called Arlington Heights and talked with the city clerk himself. No record. How about any record of Linda Hawkins or Linda Rabb? None, no birth certificate, no marriage license. If I'd wait a minute, he'd check motor vehicles. I waited. It was more like ten minutes. The air blowing in from Stuart Street was hot and gritty. The sweat had soaked through my polo shirt and made it stick to my back. I looked at my watch: 3:15. I hadn't had lunch yet. I sniffed at the hot breeze. If the wind was right, I could catch the scent of sauerbraten wafting across the street from Jake Wirth's. It wasn't right. All I could smell was the uncontrolled emission of the traffic.

The Arlington Heights city clerk came back on the phone.

"Still there?"

"Yep."

"Got no record of a driver's license. No auto registration. There's four Hawkinses in the city directory but no Linda. Want the phone numbers?"

"Yes, and can you give me the number of the school administration department?"

"Yeah, one minute, I'll check it here."

He did and gave it to me. I called them. They had no record of Linda Rabb or Linda Hawkins. There had been eight children named Hawkins in the school system since 1960. Six were boys. The other two were named Doris and Olive.

I hung up. Very cooperative.

I called the first Hawkins number in Arlington Heights. No soap. Nor was there any soap at the next two. The fourth number didn't answer. But unless they were the ones when I finally got them, I was going to have to wonder about old Linda. I looked at my watch: 4:30. Three thirty in Illinois. I hadn't eaten since breakfast. I went over to Jake Wirth's, had some sauerbraten and dark beer, came back to the office at five forty-five, and called the fourth Hawkins again. A woman answered who had never heard of Linda Hawkins.

I swung my chair around and propped my feet on the windowsill and looked out at the top floor of the garment loft across the street. It was empty. Everyone had gone home. There are a lot of reasons why someone doesn't check out right off quick when you begin to look into her background. But most of them have to do with deceit, and most deceit is based on having something to hide. Two pigeons settled down onto the window ledge

58

of the loft and looked at me looking at them. I looked at my watch: 6:10. After supper on a summer evening. Twilight softball leagues were getting under way at this hour. Kids were going out to hang out on the corner till dark. Men were watering their lawns, their wives sitting nearby in lawn chairs. I was looking at two pigeons.

Linda Rabb was not what she was supposed to be, and that bothered me, like it bothered me that she met Rabb at a ball game even though she wasn't interested in baseball till she married him. Little things, but they weren't right. The pigeons flew off. The traffic sounds were dwindling. I'd have to find out about Linda Rabb. The Sox had a night game tonight, which meant Rabb wouldn't be home. But Linda Rabb probably would be because of the kid. I called. She was.

"I wonder if I could drop by just for a minute," I said. "Just want to get the wife's angle on things. You know, what it's like to be home while the game's on, that sort of thing." What a writer I'd make, get the wife's angle. Slick. Probably should have said "little woman's angle."

"That's okay, Mr. Spenser, I'm just giving the baby his bath. If you drop around in an hour or so, I'll be watching the game on television, but we can talk."

I thanked her and hung up. I looked at the window ledge on the garment loft some more. My office door opened behind me. I swiveled the chair around. A short fat man in a Hawaiian shirt and a panama hat came in and left the door open behind him. The shirt hung outside his maroon double knit pants. He wore wrap-around black-rimmed sunglasses and smoked a cigar. He looked around my office without saying anything. I put my feet up on my desk and looked at him. He stepped aside, and another man came in and sat down in front of my desk. He was wearing a tan suit, dark brown shirt, and a wide red-striped tie in browns, whites, and yellows. His tan loafers were gleaming; his hands were manicured; his face was tanned. His hair was bright gray and expensively barbered, curling over his collar in the back, falling in a single ringlet over his forehead. Despite the gray hair, his face was young and unlined. I knew him. His name was Frank Doerr.

"I'd like to talk with you, Spenser."

"Oh golly," I said, "you heard about my whipped cream biscuits and you were hoping I'd give you the recipe."

The fat guy in the panama hat had closed the door behind Doerr and was leaning against it with his arms folded. Akim Tamiroff.

Doerr said, "You know who I am, Spenser?"

"Aren't you Julia Child?" I said.

"My name's Doerr. I want to know what business you're doing with the Red Sox."

A master of disguise, the man of 1,000 faces. "Red Sox?" I said.

"Red Sox," he said.

"Jesus, I didn't think the word would get out that quickly. How'd you find out?"

"Never mind how I found out, I want answers."

"Sure, sure thing, Mr. Doerr. You any relation to Bobby?"

"Don't irritate me, Spenser. I am used to getting answers."

"Yeah, well, I didn't know you had anything against Bobby Doerr, I thought he was a hell of a second baseman."

Doerr said, "Wally," without looking around, and the fat man at the door brought a gun out from under his flowered shirt. "Now knock off the bullshit, Spenser. I haven't got a lot of time to spend in this roach hole."

I thought "roach hole" was a little unkind, but I thought the gun in Wally's hand was a little unkind too. "Okay," I said, "no need to get sore. I was a regional winner in the Leon Culberson look-alike contest, and the

Sox wanted to talk to me about being a designated hitter."

Doerr and Wally looked at me. The silence got to be quite long. "You don't think I look like Leon Culberson?" I said.

Doerr leaned forward. "I asked around a little about you, Spenser. I heard you think you're a riot. I think you're a roach in a roach hole. I think you're a thirty-five-cent piece of hamburg, and I think you need to learn some manners."

The building was quiet; the traffic sounds were less frequent through the open window. Wally's gun pointed at me without moving. Wally sucked on one of his canine teeth. My stomach hurt a little.

Doerr went on. "You are hanging around Fenway Park, hanging around the broadcast booth, talking with people, pretending you're a writer, and not telling anyone at all that you're only a goddamned egg-sucking snoop, a nickel-and-dime cheapie. I want to know why, and I want to know right now or Wally will make you wish you'd never been born."

I took my feet off the desk, slowly, and put them on the floor. I put my hands, slowly, on the desk and stood up. When I was on my feet, I said, "Frank, baby, you're a gambling man, and I'll make a bet with you. In fact, I'll make two. First one is that you won't shoot because you want to know what's happening and what I'm into and it's lousy percentage to shoot a guy without being sure why. Second bet is that if your pet pork chop tries to hassle me, I can take away his piece and clean his teeth with it. Even money."

As far as Wally showed anything, I might have been talking about Sam Yorty or the Aga Khan. He didn't move. Neither did the gun. Doerr's sun-lamp face seemed to have gotten whiter. The lines from his nostrils to the corners of his mouth had gotten deeper, and his right eyelid tremored. My stomachache continued.

Another silence. If I weren't so tough, I would have thought maybe I was scared. Wally's gun was a Walther P.38. Nine-millimeter. Seven shots in the clip. Nice gun, the grip on a Walther was very comfortable, and the balance was good. Wally seemed happy with his. Below on Stuart Street somebody with a trick horn blew shave-and-a-haircut-two-bits. And some brakes squealed.

Doerr got up suddenly, turned on his heels, and walked out. Wally put the gun away, followed him out, and closed the door. I breathed in most of the air in the office through my nose and let it out again very slowly. My fingertips tingled. I sat down again, opened the bottom desk drawer, took out a bottle of bourbon, and drank from the neck. I coughed. I'd have to stop buying the house brand at Vito's Superette.

I looked around at the empty office. Green file cabinet, three Vermeer prints that Susan Silverman had given me for Christmas, the chair that Doerr had sat in. Didn't look so goddamned roachie to me.

7

I took a Polaroid camera with me when I visited Linda Rabb.

"I want to think about graphics, maybe a coffee table book," I told her. "Maybe a big format."

She was in blue jeans, barefoot, a ribbon in her hair, her makeup fresh. On a twenty-five-inch color console in the living room, Buck Maynard was calling the play by play. "Ah want to tell ya, Holly West could throw a lamb chop past a wolf pack, Doc. He gunned Amos Otis down by twenty feet."

"Great arm, Buck," Wilson said, "a real cannon back there."

I snapped some pictures of Linda and the living room from different angles.

"Do you get nervous watching Marty pitch, Linda?" I lay on the floor to get an exotic angle, shooting up through the glass top of the coffee table.

"No, not so much anymore. He's so good, you know — it's more, I'm surprised when he loses. But I don't worry."

"Does he bring it home or leave it at the park?"

"When he loses? He leaves it there. Unless you've been watching the game, you don't know if he won or lost when he comes in the door. He doesn't talk about it at all. Little Marty barely knows what his father does."

I placed the five color shots on the coffee table in front of Linda Rabb.

"Which one do you like best?" I said. "They're only idea shots; if the publishers decide to go the big picture format, we'll use a pro." I sounded like Arthur Author — it pays to listen to the Carson show.

She picked up the last one on the left and held it at an angle to the light.

"This is an interesting shot," she said. It was the one I'd taken from floor level. It was interesting. Casey Crime Photographer.

"Yeah, that's good," I said. "I like that one too." I took it from her and put it in an envelope. "How about the others?"

She looked at several more. "They're okay, but the one I gave you first is my favorite."

"Okay," I said. "We agree." I scooped the other four into a second envelope.

Bucky Maynard said, "We got us a real barn burner here, Doc. Both pitchers are hummin' it in there pretty good."

"You're absolutely right, Bucky. A couple of real fine arms out there tonight."

I stood up. "Thank you, Linda. I'm sorry

to have barged in on you like this."

"That's okay. I enjoyed it. The only thing is, I don't know about pictures of me, or of the baby. Marty doesn't like to have his family brought into things. I mean, we're very private people. Marty may not want you to do pictures."

"I can understand that, Linda. Don't worry. There are lots of people on the team, and if we decide to go to visuals, we can use some of them if Marty objects."

She shook my hand at the door. It was a bony hand and cold.

Outside, it was dark now, and the traffic was infrequent. I walked up Mass Ave toward the river, crossing before I got to Boylston Street to look at the Spanish melons in the window of a gourmet food shop. Mingled with the smell of automobiles and commerce were the thin, damp smell of the river and the memory of trees and soil that the city supplanted. At Marlborough I turned right and strolled down toward my apartment. The small trees and the flowering shrubs in front of the brick and brownstone buildings enhanced the river smell.

It was nine fifteen when I got in my apartment. I called the Essex County DA's office on the chance that someone might be there late. Someone was, probably an assistant DA working up a loan proposal so he could open an office and go into private practice.

"Lieutenant Healy around?" I asked.

"Nope, he's working out of ten-ten Commonwealth, temporary duty, probably be there a couple of months. Can I do anything for you?"

I said no and hung up.

I called state police headquarters at 1010 Commonwealth Ave in Boston. Healy wasn't in. Call back in the morning. I hung up and turned on the TV. Boston had a two-run lead over Kansas City. I opened a bottle of Amstel beer, lay down on my couch, and watched the ball game. John Mayberry tied the game with a one-on home run in the top of the ninth, and I went through three more Amstels before Johnny Tabor scored from third on a Holly West sacrifice fly in the eleventh inning. While the news was on, I made a Westphalian ham sandwich on pumpernickel, ate it, and drank another bottle of Amstel. A man needs sustenance before bed. I might have an exciting dream. I didn't.

Next morning I drove over to 1010 Commonwealth. Healy was in his office, his coat off, the cuffs of his white shirt turned back, but the narrow black knit tie neat and tight around the short, pointed collar. He was medium height, slim, with a gray crew cut and pale blue eyes like Paul Newman. He looked like a career man in a discount shirt store. Five years ago he had gone into a candy store unarmed and rescued two hostages from a nervous junkie with a shotgun. The only person hurt was the junkie.

He said, "What do you want, Spenser?" I was always one of his favorites.

I said, "I'm selling copies of the *Police Gazette* and thought you might wish to keep abreast of the professional developments in your field."

"Knock off the horse crap, Spenser, what do you want?"

I took out the envelope containing my Polaroid picture of Marty Rabb's coffee table.

"There's a photograph in here with two sets of prints on it. One set is mine. I want to know who the other one belongs to. Can you run it through the FBI for me?"

"Why?"

"Would you buy, I'm getting married and want to run a credit check on my bride-to-be?"

"No."

"I didn't think so. Okay. It's confidential. I don't want to tell you if I don't have to. But I gotta know, and I'll give you the reasons if you insist."

"Where do you buy your clothes, Spenser?"

69

"Aha, bribery. You want the name of my tailor, because I'm your clothing idol."

"You dress like a goddamned hippie. Don't you own a tie?"

"One," I said. "So I can eat in the main dining room at the Ritz."

"Gimme the photo," Healy said. "I'll let you know what comes back."

I gave him the envelope. "Tell your people to try and not get grape jelly and marshmallow fluff all over the photo, okay?"

Healy ignored me. I left.

Going out, I got a look at myself in the glass doors. I had on a red and black paisley sport coat, a black polo shirt, black slacks, and shiny black loafers with a crinkle finish and gold buckles. Hippie? Healy's idea of aggressive fashion was French cuffs. I put on my sunglasses, got in my car, and headed down Commonwealth toward Kenmore Square. The top was down and the seat was quite hot. Not a single girl turned to stare at me as I went by.

8

I went over to Fenway and watched the Sox get ready for an afternoon game. I talked for a half hour with Holly West and a half hour with Alex Montoya to keep up my investigative-writer image, but I wondered how long that would last. Doerr knew I was there, which meant probably that someone there knew I was not a writer. Which also meant that there was a connection between Doerr and the Sox, a connection Doerr wanted to protect. He'd made an error coming to see me. But it's the kind of error guys like Doerr are always making. They get so used to having everyone say yes to them that they forget about the chance that someone will say no. People with a lot of power get like that. They think they're omnipotent. They screw up. Doerr was so surprised that I told him and Wally to take a walk that he didn't know what else to do, so he took a walk. But the cat was now out of the valise. I had a feeling I might hear from Doerr again. It was not a soothing feeling.

I was leaning against the railing of the box seats by the Red Sox dugout, watching batting practice, when Billy Carter said, "Hey,

Spenser, want to take a few cuts?"

I did, but I couldn't take my coat off and show the gun. And I didn't want to swing with my coat on. I didn't need any handicaps. I shook my head.

"Why not? Sully's just lobbing them up," Carter said.

"I promised my mom when I took up the violin I'd never play baseball again."

"Violin? Are you shitting? You don't look like no violinist to me. How much you weigh?"

"One ninety-five, one ninety-seven, around there."

"Yeah? You work out or anything?"

"I lift a little. Run some."

"Yeah. I thought you did something. You didn't get that neck from playing no fiddle. What can you bench?"

"Two fifty."

"How many reps?"

"Fifteen."

"Hey, man, we oughta set up an arm wrestle between you and Holly. Wouldn't that be hot shit if you beat him? Man, Holly would turn blue if a goddamned writer beat him arm wrestling."

"Who's pitching today?" I asked.

"Marty," Carter said. "Who busted up your nose?"

72

"It's a long list," I said. "I used to fight once. How's Marty to catch?"

"A tit," Carter said. One of the coaches was hitting fungoes to the outfield from a circle to the right of the batting cage. The ball parabolaed out in what seemed slow motion against the high tangible sky. "A real tit. You just sit back there and put your glove on the back of the plate and Marty hits it. And you can call the game. You give a sign, Marty nods, and the pitch comes right there. He never shakes you off."

"Everything works, huh?"

"Yeah, I mean he's got the fast ball, slider, a big curve, and a change off all of them. And he can put them all up a gnat's ass at sixty feet six, you know. I mean, he's a tit to catch. If I could catch him every day, and the other guys didn't throw curves, I could be Hall of Fame, baby. Cooperstown."

"When do you think you'll catch a game, Billy?"

"Soon as Holly gets so he can't walk. Around there. Whoops . . . here comes the song of the South, old hush puppy."

Bucky Maynard had come out from under the stands and was behind the batting cage. With him was Lester, resplendent in a buckskin hunting shirt and a black cowboy hat with big silver conches on the band around the

73

crown. Maynard had swapped his red-checked shirt for a white one with green ferns on it. His arms in the short sleeves were pink with sunburn. He had the look of someone who didn't tan.

"You don't seem too fond of Maynard," I said.

"Me? I love every ounce of his cuddly little lard-assed self."

"Okay to quote you?" I wanted to see Carter's reaction.

"Jesus, no. If sowbelly gets on your ass, you'll find yourself warming up relievers in the Sally League. No shit, Spenser, I think he's got more influence around here than Farrell."

"How come?"

"I don't know. I mean, the freakin' fans love him. They think he's giving them the real scoop, you know, all the hot gossip about the big-league stars, facts you don't get on the bubble-gum card."

"Is he?"

"No, not really. He's just nasty. If he hears any gossip, he spreads it. The goddamned ya-hoos eat it up. Tell-it-like-it-is Bucky. Shit."

"What's the real story on the lizard that trails behind him?"

"Lester?"

"Yeah."

Carter shrugged. "I dunno, he drives Bucky around. He keeps people away from him. He's some kind of karate freak or whatever."

"Tae kwon do," I said. "It's Korean karate."

"Yeah, whatever. I wouldn't mess much with him either. I guess he's a real bastard. I hear he did a real tune on some guy out in Anaheim. The guy was giving Maynard some crap in the hotel bar out there and Lester the Fester damn near killed him. Hey, I gotta take some swings. Catch you later."

Carter headed for the batting cage. Clyde Sullivan, the pitching coach, was pitching batting practice, and when Carter stepped in, he turned and waved the outfielders in. "Up yours, Sully," Carter said. Maynard left the batting cage and strolled over toward me. Lester moved along bonelessly behind him.

"How you doing, Mr. Spenser?" Maynard said.

"Fine," I said. "And yourself?"

"Oh, passable, for an older gentleman. That Carter's funny as a crutch, ain't he?"

I nodded.

"Ah just wish his arm was as good as his mouth," Maynard said. "He can't throw past the pitcher's mound."

"How's his bat?"

Maynard smiled. It was not a radiant smile;

the lips pulled down over the teeth so that the smile was a toothless crescent in his red face with neither warmth nor humor suggested. "He's all right if the ball comes straight. Except the ball don't never come straight a course."

"Nice kid, though," I said. Lester had hooked both elbows over the railings and was standing with one booted foot against the wall and one foot flat on the ground. Gary Cooper. He spit a large amount of brown saliva toward the batter's cage, and I realized he was chewing tobacco. When he got into an outfit, he went all the way.

"Maybe," Maynard said, "but ah wouldn't pay much mind to what he says. He likes to run his mouth."

"Don't we all," I said. "Hell, writers and broadcasters get paid for it."

"Ah get paid for reporting what happens, Carter tends to make stuff up. There's a difference."

Maynard looked quite steadily at me, and I had the feeling we were talking about serious stuff. Lester spit another dollop of tobacco juice.

"Okay by me," I said. "I'm just here listening and thinking. I'm not making any judgments yet."

"What might you be making judgments

about, Spenser?"

"What to include, what to leave out, what seems to be the truth, what seems to be fertilizer. Why do you ask?"

"Just interested. Ah like to know a man, and one way is to know how he does his job. Ah'm just lookin' into how you do yours."

"Fair enough," I said. "I'll be looking into how you do yours in a bit." Veiled innuendo, that's the ticket, Spenser. Subtle.

"Long as you don't interfere, ah'll be happy to help. Who'd you say was your publisher?"

"Subsidy," I said. "Subsidy Press, in New York."

Maynard looked at his watch. It was one of those that you press a button and the time is given as a digital readout. "Well, time for the Old Buckaroo to get on up to the booth. Nice talking to you, Spenser."

He waddled off, his feet splayed, the toes pointing out at forty-five-degree angles. Lester unhinged and slouched after him, eyes alert under the hatbrim for lurking rustlers. There never was a man like Shane. Tomorrow he'd probably be D'Artagnan.

There'd been some fencing going on there, more than there should have been. It was nearly one. I went down into the locker room and used the phone on Farrell's desk to call Brenda Loring at work.

"I have for you, my dear, a proposition," I said.

"I know," she said. "You make it every time I see you."

"Not that proposition," I said. "I have an additional one, though that previously referred to above should not be considered thereby inoperative."

"I beg your pardon?"

"I didn't understand that either," I said. "Look, here's my plan. If you can get the afternoon off, I will escort you to the baseball game, buy you some peanuts and Cracker Jacks, and you won't care if you ever come back."

"Do I get dinner afterwards?"

"Certainly and afterwards we can go to an all-night movie and neck. What do you say?"

"Oh, be still my heart," she said. "Shall I meet you at the park?"

"Yeah, Jersey Street entrance. You'll recognize me at once by the cluster of teeny-boppers trying to get me to autograph their bras."

"I'll hurry," she said.

9

When Brenda Loring got out of a brown and white Boston cab, I was brushing off an old man in an army shirt and a flowered tie who wanted me to give him a quarter.

"Did you autograph his bra, sweetie?" she said.

"They were here," I said, "but I warned them about your jealous passion and they fled at your approach."

"Fled? That is quite fancy talk for a professional thug."

"That's another thing. Around here I'm supposed to be writing a book. My true identity must remain concealed. Reveal it to no one."

"A writer?"

"Yeah. I'm supposed to be doing a book on the Red Sox and baseball."

"Was that your agent you were talking with when I drove up?"

"No, a reader."

She shook her head. Her blond hair was cut short and shaped around her head. Her eyes were green. Her makeup was expert. She was wearing a short green dress with a small floral print and long sleeves. She was darkly tanned, and a small gold locket gleamed on a thin chain against her chest where the neckline of the dress formed a V. Across Jersey Street a guy selling souvenirs was staring at her. I was staring at her too. I always did. She was ten pounds on the right side of plump. "Voluptuous," I said.

"I beg your pardon."

"That's how we writers would describe you. Voluptuous with a saucy hint of deviltry lurking in the sparkling of the eyes and the impertinent cast of the mouth."

"Spenser, I want a hot dog and some beer and peanuts and a ball game. Could you please, please, please, pretty please, please with sugar on it knock off the writer bullshit and escort me through the gate?"

I shook my head. "Writers aren't understood much," I said, and we went in.

I was showing off for Brenda and took her up to the broadcast booth to watch the game. My presence didn't seem to be a spur to the Red Sox. They lost to Kansas City 5–2, with Freddie Patek driving in three runs on a bases-loaded fly ball that Alex Montoya played into a triple. Maynard ignored us, Wilson studied Brenda closely between innings, and Lester boned up on the *National Enquirer* through the whole afternoon. Thoughtful.

It was four ten when we got out onto Jersey Street again. Brenda said, "Who was the cute thing in the cowboy suit?"

"Never mind about him," I said. "I suppose you're not going to settle for the two hot dogs I bought you."

"For dinner? I'll wait right here for the cowboy."

"Where would you like to go? It's early, but we could stop for a drink."

We decided on a drink at the outdoor café by City Hall. I had draft beer, and Brenda a stinger on the rocks, under the colorful umbrellas across from the open brick piazza. The area was new, reclaimed from the miasma of Scollay Square where Winnie Garrett the Flaming Redhead used to take it all off on the first show Monday before the city censor decreed the G-string. Pinball parlors, and tattoo shops, the Old Howard and the Casino, winos, whores, sailors, barrooms, and novelty shops: an adolescent vision of Sodom and Gomorrah, all gone now, giving way to fountains and arcades and a sweep of open plaza.

"You know, it never really was Sodom and Gomorrah anyway," I said.

"What wasn't?"

"Scollay Square. It was pre-Vietnam sin. Burlesque dancers and barrooms where bleached blondes danced in G-strings and net stockings. Places that sold plastic dog turds and whoopee cushions."

"I never came here," she said. "My mother had me convinced that to step into Scollay Square was to be molested instantly."

"Naw. There were ten college kids here for every dirty old man. Compared to the Combat Zone, Scollay Square was the Goosie Gander Nursery School."

I ordered two more drinks. The tables were glass-topped and the café was carpeted in Astroturf. The waitress was attentive. Brenda Loring's nails were done in a bright red. Dark was still a long way off.

Brenda went to the ladies' room, and I called my answering service. There was a message to call Healy. He'd be in his office till six. I looked at my watch: 5:40. I called.

"This is Spenser, what have you got?"

"Prints belong to Donna Burlington." He spelled it. "Busted in Redford, Illinois, three-eighteen-sixty-six, for possession of a prohibited substance. That's when the prints got logged into the bureau files. No other arrests recorded."

"Thanks, Lieutenant."

"You owe me," Healy said and hung up. Mr. Warmth.

I was back at the table before Brenda.

At seven fifteen we strolled up Tremont Street to a French restaurant in the old City Hall and had rack of lamb for two and a chilled bottle of Traminer and strawberry tarts for dessert. It was nearly nine thirty when we finished and walked back up School Street to Tremont. It was dark now but still warm, a soft night, midsummer, and the Common seemed very gentle as we strolled across it. Brenda Loring held my hand as we walked. No one attempted to mug us all the way to Marlborough Street.

In my apartment I said to Brenda, "Want some brandy or would you like to get right to the necking?"

"Actually, cookie, I would like first to take a shower."

"A shower?"

"Uh-huh. You pour us two big snifters of brandy and hop into bed, and I'll come along in a few minutes."

"A shower?"

"Go on," she said. "I won't take long."

I went to the kitchen and got a bottle of Rémy Martin out of the kitchen cabinet. Did David Niven keep cognac in the kitchen? Not likely. I got two brandy snifters out and filled them half full and headed back toward the bedroom. I could hear the shower running. I put the two glasses down on the bureau and got undressed. The shower was still running. I went to the bathroom door. My bare feet made no noise at all on the wall-to-wall carpeting. I turned the handle and it opened. The room was steamy. Brenda's clothes were in a small pile on the floor under the sink. I noticed her lingerie matched her dress. Class. The steam was billowing up over the drawn shower curtain. I looked in. Brenda had her eyes closed, her head arched back, the water running down over her shiny brown body. Her buttocks were in white contrast to the rest of her. She was humming an old Billy Eckstine song. I got in behind her and put my arms around her.

"Jesus Christ, Spenser," she said. "What are you doing?"

"Cleanliness is next to godliness," I said. "Want me to wash your back?"

She handed me the soap and I lathered her back. When I was finished, she turned to rinse it off, and her breasts, as she faced me, were the same startling white that her buttocks had been.

"Want me to wash your front?" I said.

She laughed and put her arms around me. Her body was slick and wet. I kissed her. There is excitement in a new kiss, but there is a quality of memory and intimacy in kissing someone you've kissed often before. I liked the quality. Maybe continuity is better than change. With the shower still running we went towelless to bed.

10

Ten hours later I was in the coach section, window seat, aft of the wing, in an American Airlines 747, sipping coffee and chewing with little pleasure a preheated bun that tasted vaguely of adhesive tape. We were passing over Buffalo, which was a good idea, and heading for Chicago.

Beside me was a kid, maybe fiiteen, and his brother, maybe eleven. They were discussing somebody named Ben, who might have been a dog, laughing like hell about it. Their mother and father across the aisle took turns giving them occasional warning glances when the laughter got raucous. Their mother looked like she might be a fashion designer or a lady lawyer; the old man looked like a stevedore, uncomfortable in a shirt and tie. Beauty and the beast.

We got into Chicago at eleven. I rented a car, got a road map from the girl at the rental agency counter, and drove southwest from Chicago toward Redford, Illinois. It took six and a half hours, and the great heartland of America was hot as hell. My green rental Dodge had air conditioning and I kept it at full blast all the way. About two thirty I stopped at a diner and had two cheeseburgers and a black coffee. There was a blackberry pie which the counterman claimed his wife made, and I ate two pieces. He had married well. About four thirty the highway bent south and I saw the river. I'd seen it before, but each time I felt the same tug. The Mississippi, Cartier and La Salle, Grant at Vicksburg and "it's lovely to live on a raft." A mile wide and "just keeps rolling." I pulled up onto the shoulder of the highway and looked at it for maybe five minutes. It was brown and placid.

I got to Redford at twenty of seven and checked into a two-story Holiday Inn just north of town that offered a view of the river and a swimming pool. The dining room was open and more than half empty. I ordered a draft beer and looked at the menu. The beer came in an enormous schooner. I ordered Wiener schnitzel and fresh garden vegetables and was startled to find when it came that it was excellent. I had finished two of the enormous schooners by then and perhaps my palate was insensitive to nuance. My compliments to the chef. Three stars for the Holiday Inn in Redford, Illinois. I signed the check and went to bed.

The next morning I went into town. Outside the air-conditioned motel the air was hot with a strong river smell. Cicadas hummed. The Holiday Inn and the Mississippi River were obviously Redford's high spots. It was a very small town, barely more than a cluster of shabby frame houses along the river. The yards were mostly bare dirt with an occasional clump of coarse and ratty-looking grass. The town's single main street contained a hardware and feed store, a Woolworth's five-and-ten, Scooter's Lunch, Bill and Betty's Market with two Phillips 66 pumps out front, and, fronting on a small square of dandelion-spattered grass, the yellow clapboard two-story town hall. There were two Greek Revival columns holding up the overhanging second floor and a bell tower that extended up perhaps two more stories to a thin spire with a weathervane at the tip. In the small square were a nineteenth-century cannon and a pyramid of cannonballs. Two kids were sitting astride the cannon as I pulled up in front of the town hall. In the parking area to the right of the town hall was a black and white Chevy with a whip antenna and POLICE lettered on the side. I went around to that side and down along the building. In the back was a screen door with a small blue light over it. I went in.

There was a head-high standing floor fan at the long end of a narrow room, and it blew a steady stream of hot air at me. To my right was a low mahogany dividing rail, and behind it a gray steel desk and matching swivel chair, a radio receiver-transmitter and a table mike on a maple table with claw and ball feet, a white round-edged refrigerator with gold trim, and some wanted posters fixed to the door with magnets. And a gray steel file cabinet.

A gray-haired man with rimless glasses and a screaming eagle emblem tattooed on his right forearm was sitting at the desk with his arms folded across his chest and his feet up. He had on a khaki uniform, obviously starched, and his black engineer boots gleamed with polish. A buff-colored campaign hat lay on the desk beside an open can of Dr Pepper. On a wheel-around stand next to the radio equipment a portable black-and-white television was showing *Hollywood Squares*. A nameplate on the desk said T. P. DONALDSON. A big silver star on his shirt said SHERIFF. A brown cardboard bakery box on the desk contained what looked like some lemon-filled doughnuts.

"My name's Spenser," I said, and showed the photostat of my license in its clear plastic coating. Germ-free. "I'm trying to backtrack a woman named Donna Burlington. According to the FBI records she was arrested here in nineteen sixty-six."

"Sheriff Donaldson," the gray-haired man said, and stood up to shake hands. He was tall and in shape with healthy color to his tan face, and oversize hands with prominent knuckles. His shirt was ironed in a military press and had been tailored down so that it was skintight.

"Hundred and First?" I said.

"The tattoo? Yeah. I was a kid then, you know. Fulla piss and vinegar, drunk in London, and three of us got it done. My wife's always telling me to get rid of it but . . ." He shrugged. "You airborne?"

"Nope, infantry and a different war. But I remember the Hundred and First. Were you at Bastogne?"

"Yep. Had a bad case of boils on my back. The medics said I ought to eat better food and wash more often." His face was solemn. "Krauts took care of it, though. I got a back full of shrapnel and the boils were gone."

"Medical science," I said.

He shook his head. "Christ, that was thirty years ago."

"It's one of the things you don't forget," I said.

"You don't for sure," he said. "Who was that you were after?"

"Burlington, Donna Burlington. A.k.a. Linda Hawkins, about twenty-six years old, five feet four, black hair, FBI records show she was fingerprinted here in nineteen sixty-six, at which time she would have been about eighteen. You here then?"

He nodded. "Yep, I been here since nineteen forty-six." He turned toward the file cabinet. A pair of handcuffs draped over his belt in the small of his back, and he wore an army .45 in a government-issue flap holster on his right hip. He rustled through the third file drawer down and came up with a manila folder. He opened it, his back still to me, and read through the contents, closed it, turned around, put the folder facedown on the desk, and sat down. "You want a Dr Pepper?" he said.

"No, thanks. You have Donna Burlington?"

"Could I see your license again, and maybe some other ID?"

I gave him the license and my driver's license. He looked at them carefully and turned them back to me. "Why do you want to know about Donna Burlington?"

"I don't want to tell you. I'm looking into something that might hurt a lot of people, who could turn out to be innocent, if the word got out."

"What's Donna Burlington got to do with it?"

"She lied to me about her name, where she

lived, how she got married. I want to know why."

"You think she's committed a crime?"

"Not that I know of. I don't want her for anything. I just ran across a lie and I want to run it down. You know how it goes, people lie to you, you want to know why."

Donaldson nodded. He took a swig from his Dr Pepper, swallowed it, and began to suck on his upper lip.

"I don't want to stir up old troubles," I said. "She was eighteen when you busted her. Everyone is entitled to screw up when they're eighteen. I just want to know about her."

Donaldson kept sucking on his upper lip and looking at me.

"It'll be worse if I start asking around and get people wondering why some dick from the East is asking about Donna Burlington. I'll find out anyway. This isn't that big a place."

"I might not let you ask around," Donaldson said.

"Aw come on, Hondo," I said. "If you give me trouble, I'll go get the state cops and a court order and come on back and ask around and more people will notice and a bigger puff of smoke will go up and you'll be worse off than you are now. I'm making what you call your legitimate inquiry."

"Persistent sonovabitch, aren't you? Okay, I'll go along. I just don't like telling people's business to others without a pretty good reason."

"Me either," I said.

"Okay." He opened the folder and looked at it. "I arrested Donna Burlington for possession of three marijuana cigarettes. She was smoking with two boys from Buckston in a pickup truck back of Scooter's Lunch. It was a first offense, but we were a little jumpier about reefers around here in 'sixty-six than we are now. I booked her; she went to court and got a suspended sentence and a year's probation. Six weeks later she broke probation and went off to New York City with a local hellion. She never came back."

"What was the hellion's name?"

"Tony Reece. He was about seven or eight years older than Donna."

"What kind of kid was she?"

"It was a while ago," Donaldson said. "But kind of restless, not really happy, you know — nothing bad, but she had a reputation, hung out with the older hotshots. The first girl in class to smoke, the first to drink, the first one to try pot, the one the boys took out as soon as they dared while the other girls were still going to dancing school at the grange hall and blushing if someone talked dirty."

"Family still live in town?"

"Yeah, but they don't know where she is. After she took off, they were after me to locate her. But there's only me and two deputies, and one of them's part-time. When nothing came of that, they wrote her off. In a way they were probably glad she took off. They didn't know what to do with her. She was a late baby, you know? The Burlingtons never had any kids, and then, when Mrs. Burlington was going through the change, there came Donna. That's what my wife says anyway. Embarrassed the hell out of both of them."

"How about Reece? He ever show up again?"

Donaldson shook his head. "Nope. I heard he got in some kind of jam in New York and he might be doing time. But he hasn't shown up around here anyway."

"Okay, any last known address?"

"Just the house here."

"Can you give me that? I'd like to talk to the parents."

"I'll drive you over. They'll be a little easier if I'm there. They're old and they get nervous."

"I'm not going to give them the third degree, Donaldson, I'm just going to talk to them and ask them if they know anything more than you do about Donna Burlington."

"I'll go along. They're sorta shiftless and crummy, but they're my people, you know? I like to look out for them."

I nodded. "Okay, let's go."

We got into Donaldson's black and white and drove back up the main street past the row of storefronts and the sparse yards. At the end of the street we turned left, down toward the river, and pulled up in front of a big shanty. Originally it had probably been a four-room bungalow backing onto the river. Over the years lean-tos and sagging additions had been scabbed onto it so that it was difficult to say how many rooms there were now. The area in front of the house was mud, and several dirty white chickens pecked in it. A brown and white pig had rooted itself out a hollow against the foundation and was sleeping in it. To the right of the front door, two big gas bottles of dull gray-green metal stood upright, and to the left the remnants of a vine were so bedraggled I couldn't recognize what kind it was. The land to the side and rear of the house sloped in a kind of eroded gully down to the river. There was a stack of old tires at the corner of one of the lean-tos, and beyond that the rusted frame of a forty-year-old pickup truck, a stack of empty vegetable crates, and on the flat mud margin where the river lapped at the land a bedspring, mossy and slick with river scum.

I thought of Linda Rabb in her Church Park apartment with the fresh jeans and her black hair gleaming.

"Come to where the flavor is," I said.

"Yeah, it's not much, is it? Don't much wonder that Donna took off as soon as she could." We got up and walked to the front door. There were the brown remains of a wreath hanging from a galvanized nail. The ghost of Christmas past. Maybe of a Christmas future for the Burlingtons.

An old woman answered Donaldson's knock. She was fat and lumpy in a yellow housedress. Her legs were bare and mottled, her feet thrust into scuffed men's loafers. Her gray hair was short and straight around her head, the ends uneven, cut at home probably, with dull scissors. Her face was nearly without features, fat puffing around her eyes, making them seem small and squinty.

"Morning, Mrs. Burlington," Donaldson said. "Got a man here from Boston wants to talk with you about Donna."

She looked at me. "You seen Donna?" she said.

"May we come in?" I said.

She stood aside. "I guess so," she said. Her voice wasn't very old, but it was without variation, a tired monotone, as if there were nothing worth saying.

Donaldson took off his hat and went in. I followed. The room smelled of kerosene and dogs and things I didn't recognize. The clutter was dense. Donaldson and I found room on an old daybed and sat. Mrs. Burlington shuffled off down a corridor and returned in a moment with her husband. He was pallid and bald, a tall old man in a sleeveless undershirt and black worsted trousers with the fly open. His face had gray stubble on it, and some egg was dried in the corner of his mouth. The skin was loose on his thin white arms and wrinkled in the fold at the armpit. He poured a handful of Bond Street pipe tobacco from a can into the palm of his hand and slurped it into his mouth.

He nodded at Donaldson, who said, "Morning, Mr. Burlington." Mrs. Burlington stood, and they both looked at Donaldson and me without moving or speaking. American Gothic.

I said, "I'm a detective. I can't tell you where your daughter is, except that she's well and happy. But I need to learn a little about her background. I mean her no harm, and I'm trying to help her, but the whole situation is very confidential."

"What do you want to know?" Mrs. Burlington said.

"When is the last time you heard from her?"

Mrs. Burlington said, "We ain't. Not since she run off."

"No letter, no call, nothing. Not a word?"

Mrs. Burlington shook her head. The old man made no move, changed his expression not at all.

"Do you know where she went when she left here?"

"Left us a note saying she was going to New York with a fellow we never met, never heard nothing more."

"Didn't you look for her?"

Mrs. Burlington nodded at Donaldson, "Told T.P. here. He looked. Couldn't find her." A bony mongrel dog with short yellow fur and mismatched ears appeared behind Mr. Burlington. He growled at us, and Burlington turned and kicked him hard in the ribs. The dog yelped and disappeared.

"You ever hear from Tony Reece?" It was like talking to a postoperative lobotomy case. And compared to the old man, she was animated.

She shook her head. "Never seen him," she said. The old man squirted a long stream of tobacco juice at a cardboard box of sand behind the door. He missed.

And that was it. They didn't know anything about anything, and they didn't care. The old man never spoke while I was there and just nodded when Donaldson said good-bye.

In the car Donaldson said, "Where to now?"

"Let's just sit here a minute until I catch my breath."

"They been poor all their life," Donaldson said. "It tends to wear you out." I nodded.

"Okay, how about Tony Reece? He got any family here?"

"Nope. Folks are both dead." Donaldson started the engine and turned the car back toward the town hall. When we got there, he offered me his hand. "If I was you, Spenser, I'd try New York next."

"Fun City," I said.

11

It was sunset when the plane swung in over the water and landed at La Guardia Airport. I took the bus into the East Side terminal at Thirty-eighth Street and a cab from there to the Holiday Inn at West Fifty-seventh Street. The Wiener schnitzel had been so good in Redford, I thought I might as well stay with a winner.

The West Side hadn't gotten any more fashionable since I had been there last and the hotel looked as if it belonged where it was. The lobby was so discouraging that I didn't bother to check the dining room for Wiener schnitzel. Instead, I walked over to a Scandinavian restaurant on Fifty-eighth Street and ravaged its smorgasbord.

The next morning I made some phone calls to the New York Department of Social Services while I drank coffee in my room. When I finished I walked along Fifty-seventh Street to Fifth Avenue and headed downtown. I always walk in New York. In the window of F.A.O. Schwarz was an enormous stuffed giraffe, and Brentano's had a display of ethnic cookbooks in the window. I thought about going in and asking them if they were a branch of the Boston store but decided not to. They probably lacked my zesty sense of humor.

It was about nine forty-five when I reached Thirty-fourth Street and turned left. Four blocks east, between Third and Second avenues, was a three-story beige brick building that looked like a modified fire station. The brown metal entrance doors, up four stairs, were flanked with flagpoles at right angles to the building. A plaque under the right-hand flagpole said CITY OF NEW YORK, DEPARTMENT OF SOCIAL SERVICES, YORKVILLE INCOME MAINTENANCE CENTER. I went in.

It was a big open room, the color a predictable green; molded plastic chairs in red, green, and blue stood three rows deep to the right of the entrance. To the left a low counter. Behind the counter a big black woman with blue-framed glasses on a chain around her neck was telling an old woman in an ankle-length dress that her check would come next week and would not come sooner. The woman protested in broken English, and the woman behind the desk said it again, louder. At the end of the counter, sitting in a folding chair, was a New York City cop, a slim black woman with badge, gun, short hair, and enormous high platform shoes. Beyond the counter the room L'd to the left, and I could see office space partitioned off. There was no one else on the floor.

Behind me, to the right of the entry, a stair led up. A handprinted sign said FACE TO FACE UPSTAIRS with an arrow. I went up. The second floor had been warrened off into cubicles where face to face could go on in privacy. The first cubicle was busy; the second was not. I knocked on the frame of the open door and went in. It was little bigger than a confessional, just a desk, a file cabinet, and a chair for the face to face. The woman at the desk was lean and young, not long out of Vassar or Bennington. She had a tanned outdoor face, with small lines around the eyes that she wasn't supposed to get yet. She had on a white sleeveless blouse open at the neck. Her brown hair was cut short and she wore no makeup. Her face presented an expression of no-nonsense compassion that I suspected she was still working on. The sign on her desk said MS. HARRIS.

"Come in," she said, her hands resting on the neat desk in front of her. A pencil in the right one. I was dressed for New York in my wheat-colored summer suit, dark blue shirt, and a white tie with blue and gold stripes. Would she invite me to her apartment? Maybe she thought I was another welfare case. If so, I'd have to speak with my tailor. I gave her a card; she frowned down at it for about thirty seconds and then looked up and said, "Yes?"

"Do you think I ought to have a motto on it?" I said.

"I beg your pardon?"

"A motto," I said. "On the card. You know, like 'We never sleep' or maybe 'Trouble is my business.' Something like that."

"Mr." — she checked the card — "Spenser, I assume you're joking and there's nothing wrong with that, but I have a good deal to do and I wonder if you might tell me what you want directly?"

"Yes, ma'am. May I sit?"

"Please do."

"Okay, I'm looking for a young woman who might have showed up here and gone on welfare about eight years ago."

"Why do you want to find her?"

I shook my head. "It's a reasonable question, but I can't tell you."

She frowned at me the way she had frowned at my card. "Why do you think we'd have information about something that far back?"

"Because you are a government agency. Government agencies never throw anything away because someone someday might need something to cover himself in case a question of responsibility was raised. You got welfare records for Peter Stuyvesant."

The frown got more severe, making a groove between her eyebrows. "Why do you think this young woman was on welfare?"

"You shouldn't frown like that," I said. "You'll get little premature wrinkles in the corners of your eyes."

"I would prefer it, Mr. Spenser, if you did not attempt to personalize this contact. The condition of my eyes is not relevant to this discussion."

"Ah, but how they sparkle when you're angry," I said.

She almost smiled, caught herself, and got the frown back in place. "Answer my question, please."

"She was about eighteen; she ran away from a small midwestern town with the local bad kid, who probably ditched her after they got here. She's a good bet to have ended up on welfare or prostitution or both. I figured that you'd have better records than Diamond Nell's Parlor of Delight."

The pencil in her right hand went tap-tap-tap on the desk. Maybe six taps before she heard it and stopped. "The fact of someone's presence on welfare rolls has sometimes been used against them. Cruel as that may seem, it is a fact of life, and I hope you can understand my reticence in this matter."

"I'm on the girl's side," I said.

"But I have no way to know that."

"Just my word," I said.

"But I don't know if your word is good."

"That's true," I said. "You don't."

The pencil went tap-tap-tap again. She looked at the phone. Pass the buck? She looked away. Good for her. "What is the girl's name?"

"Donna Burlington." I could hear a typewriter in one of the other cubicles and footsteps down another corridor. "Go ahead," I said. "Do it. It will get done by someone. It's only a matter of who. Me? Cops? Courts? Your boss? His boss? Why not you? Less fuss."

She nodded her head. "Yes. You are probably right. Very well." She got up and left the room. She had very nice legs.

It took a while. I stood in the window of the cubicle and looked down on Thirty-fourth Street and watched the people coming and going from the welfare office. It wasn't as busy as I'd thought it would be. Nor were the people as shabby. Down the corridor a man swore rapidly in Spanish. The typewriter had stopped. The rest was silence.

Ms. Harris returned with a file folder. She sat, opened it on the desk, and read the papers in it. "Donna Burlington was on income maintenance at this office from August to November nineteen sixty-six. At the time her address

105

was One Sixteen East Thirteenth Street. Her relationship with this office ended on November thirteenth, nineteen sixty-six, and I have no further knowledge of her." She closed the folder and folded her hands on top of it.

I said, "Thank you very much."

She said, "You're welcome."

I looked at my watch: 10:50. "Would you like to join me for an early lunch?" I said.

"No, thank you," she said. So much for the operator down from Boston.

"Would you like to see me do a one-hand push-up?" I said.

"Certainly not," she said. "If you have nothing more, Mr. Spenser, I have a good deal of work to do."

"Oh, sure, okay. Thanks very much for your trouble." She stood as I left the room. From the corridor I stuck my head back into the office and said, "Not everyone can do a one-hand push-up, you know?"

She seemed unimpressed and I left.

12

Thirteenth Street was a twenty-five-minute walk downtown and 116 was in the East Village between Second and Third. There was a group of men outside 116, leaning against the parked cars with their shirts unbuttoned, smoking cigarettes and drinking beer from quart bottles. They were speaking Spanish. One Sixteen was a four-story brick house, which had long ago been painted yellow and from which the paint peeled in myriad patches. Next to it was a six-story four-unit apartment building newly done in light gray paint with the door and window frames and the fire escapes and the railing along the front steps a bright red. The beer drinkers had a portable radio that played Spanish music very loudly.

I went up the four steps to number 116 and rang the bell marked CUSTODIAN. Nothing happened, and I rang it again.

One of the beer drinkers said, "Don't work, man. Who you want?"

"I want the manager."

"Inside, knock on the first door."

"Thanks."

In the entry was an empty bottle of Boone's Farm apple wine and a sneaker without laces. Stairs led up against the left wall ahead of me, and a brief corridor went back into the building to the right of the stairs. I knocked on the first door and a woman answered the first knock.

She was tall and strongly built, olive skin and short black hair. A gray streak ran through her hair from the forehead back. She had on a man's white shirt and cutoff jeans. Her feet were bare, and her toenails were painted a dark plum color. She looked about forty-five.

I said, "My name is Spenser. I'm a private detective from Boston, and I'm looking for a girl who lived here once about eight years ago."

She smiled and her teeth were very white and even. "Come in," she said. The room was large and square, and a lot of light came in through the high windows that faced out onto the street. The walls and ceiling were white, and there were red drapes at the windows and a red rug on the floor. In the middle of the room stood a big, square, thick-legged wooden table with a red linoleum top, a large bowl of fruit in the center and a high-backed wooden chair at either end. She gestured toward one of the chairs. "Coffee?" she said.

"Yes, thank you."

I sat at the table and looked about the room while she disappeared through a bead-curtained archway to make the coffee. There was a red plush round-back Victorian sofa with mahogany arms in front of the windows and an assortment of Velázquez prints on the wall. She came back in with a carafe of coffee and two white china mugs on a round red tray.

"Cream or sugar?"

I shook my head. She poured the coffee into the cups, gave me one, and sat down at the other end of the table.

"The coffee is wonderful," I said.

"I grind it myself," she said. "My name is Rose Estrada. How can I help you?" There was a very small trace of another language in her speech.

I took out the picture of Linda Rabb that I'd taken at her apartment. "This is a recent picture of a girl named Donna Burlington. In nineteen sixty-six, from August to November, she lived at this address. Can you tell me anything about her?"

She thought aloud as she looked at the picture. "Nineteen sixty-six, my youngest would have been ten. . . . Yes, I remember her, Donna Burlington. She came from somewhere in the Midwest. She seemed very young to be alone in New York, far from home. She was with a boy for a little while, but he didn't stay."

"What happened to her when she left you, do you know?"

"No."

"No forwarding address?"

"None. I remember she had no money and was behind in her rent, and I sent her down to the welfare people on Thirty-fourth Street. And then one day she gave me all the back room rent in cash and moved out."

"Any idea where she got the money?"

"I think she was hustling."

"Prostitute?"

She nodded. "I can't be sure, but I know she was out often and she brought men home often and she used to spend time with a pimp named Violet."

"Is he still around?"

"Oh sure. People like Violet are around forever."

"Where do I find him?"

"He's usually on Third Avenue, in front of the Casa Grande near Fifteenth."

"What's his full name?"

She shrugged. "Just Violet," she said. "More coffee?"

"Thank you." I held my cup out, and she poured from the carafe. Her hands were strong and clean, the fingernails the same plum color as her toenails. No rings. Outside I could hear the portable radio playing and occasionally the voices of the men drinking beer.

"She was a very small, thin, little girl," Rose Estrada said. "Very scared. She didn't want to be here, but she didn't want to go home. She didn't know anything about makeup or clothes. She didn't know what to say to people. If she was turning tricks, it must have been very hard on her."

I finished my coffee and stood. "Thank you for the coffee and for the information," I said.

"Is she in trouble?"

"No, I don't think so," I said. "Nothing I can't get her out of."

We shook hands and I left. The street seemed hot and noisy after Rose Estrada's apartment. I walked the half block to Third Ave and turned uptown. At the corner of Fourteenth Street a man in a covert cloth overcoat was urinating against the brick wall of a variety store. He was having trouble standing and lurched against the wall, holding his coat around him with one hand. Modesty, I thought, if you're going to whiz on a wall, do it with modesty. A few feet downstream another man was lying on the sidewalk, knees bent, eyes closed. Drinking buddies. I looked at my watch, it was two thirty in the afternoon.

At the corner of Fifteenth Street was a bar

with a fake fieldstone front below a plate glass window. The entry to the left of the window was imitation oak. A small neon sign said CASA GRANDE, BEER ON DRAFT. At the curb in front of the Casa Grande were a white Continental and a maroon Coupe de Ville with a white vinyl roof. Leaning against the Coupe de Ville was a man who'd seen too many *Superfly* movies. He was a black man probably six-three in his socks and about six-seven in the open-toed red platform shoes he was wearing. He was also wearing red-and-black argyle socks, black knickers, and a chain mail vest. A black Three Musketeers' hat with an enormous red plume was tipped forward over his eyes. Subtle. All he lacked was a sign saying THE PIMP IS IN.

"Excuse me," I said, "I'm looking for Violet."

The pimp looked down at me from on top of his shoes and said, "Why?"

"I was told he could give me information about a girl."

"Someone's talking shit to you, man. I don't know nothing about no girl."

"You Violet?"

He shrugged and looked down Third Avenue.

"I'm looking for information about a girl named Donna Burlington," I said.

The Lincoln started up, backed away from the curb, U-turned, and drove away.

"You federal?" Violet said. "I ain't seen you around."

"I'm not anything," I said. "Just a guy looking to buy some information."

"Well, I hope you got a license for that piece on your right hip then."

Violet paid attention to detail. "Okay." I took a card from my breast pocket and gave it to him. "I'm a private cop. From Boston. But I'm still buying information."

"Baaahston." Violet laughed. "Shit. What Donna do, steal some beans?"

"No, she stole some teenybopper clothes from a ladies' dress shop and I think you're wearing some of them."

Violet laughed again. "Hey, man, you want me to dress like one of you tight-assed honkies?" He slapped one hand down on the hood of the Cadillac and whooped with laughter. "Look at that little mother-loving Buster Brown suit. Shit." Tears were forming in his eyes.

"Look, Violet," I said. "I didn't come down here to write a sonnet about your Easter bonnet. How about I buy you a beer and we talk a little?"

"Yeah, why not, man? You said something about buying information?"

We went in the Casa Grande and sat at the bar. There was a Mets game on television down the bar. The bartender, a middle-aged man in a clean white shirt who looked like Gilbert Roland, came down and wiped the bar off in front of us.

"What'll it be, gentlemen?" he asked, looking carefully at a spot between my head and Violet's.

"Two drafts," I said.

Violet said, "Be cool, Hec, he's okay. We just talking a little business."

The bartender looked at me then. "Okay, Violet," he said and drew the beers.

Violet took his hat off. His head was stark bald and smooth. "Hec figured you for fuzz too. I hope you don't think you're working in disguise, man."

I shook my head. "You either," I said. Violet whooped again.

"What you want to know, man?"

I took out my picture of Donna Burlington and showed it to Violet. "Know her eight years younger?"

"You mentioned buying. How much you buying for?"

"Fifty bucks."

"That's not much bread, man."

"You don't have to work very hard for it," I said. "It'll cover your next tankful in that

114

brontosaurus out front."

Violet nodded, drank half his beer, and said, "Yeah, I remember Donna. Remembered her when you said her name."

"Tell me about her."

"A shit kicker," Violet said. "Come from somewhere out in the woods. Real young when she worked for me. Worked for me maybe six months."

"How'd you meet her?"

"Her boyfriend was pimping her on my turf, man. I chased him off and she stayed with me."

"She have any choice?"

Violet grinned. "Not in this neighborhood, man."

"How come you remember her so well?"

"She was white, man. Most of my chicks are black."

"What happened to her?"

Violet shrugged. "Moved uptown, fancy stuff, appointment only." He finished the beer. The bartender brought us two more without being asked.

"She work on her own?"

"Naw, she work for another broad, a madame, baby. Very classy. Probably screwed only Baaahston dudes, dig?" And again the whooping laugh.

"Can you give me the name?"

"I can get it, but that's extra."

"Another fifty?"

"That's cool." Violet got up and went to a pay phone by the door. He was back in five minutes. "Patricia Utley," he said. "Fifty-seven East Thirty-seventh Street."

"Thanks, Violet," I took a $100 bill out of my wallet and handed it to him. "If you're ever in Boston . . ."

Violet laughed again. "Yeah, baby, if I ever want some beans . . ."

I finished the beer and got up. Violet turned and leaned his elbows on the bar. "Hey, Spenser," he said. "Utley works for very heavy people, dig?"

"That's okay," I said. "I don't mind heavy work."

"Well, you built for it, I give you that. But you walk around Utley careful, baby, this ain't Boston."

"Violet," I said, "I'm not sure this is even earth."

13

Midtown East Side in Manhattan is the New York they show in the movies. Elegant, charming, clean, "I bought you violets for your furs." Patricia Utley occupied a four-story town house on East Thirty-seventh, west of Lexington. The building was stone, painted a Colonial gray with a wrought-iron filigree on the glass door and the windows faced in white. Two small dormers protruded from the slate mansard roof, and a tiny terrace to the right of the front door bloomed with flowers against the green of several miniature trees. Red geraniums and white patient Lucys in black iron pots lined the three granite steps that led up to the front door.

A well-built man with gray hair and a white mess jacket answered my ring. I gave him my card. "For Patricia Utley," I said.

"Come in, please," he said and stepped aside. I entered a center hall with a polished flagstone floor and a mahogany staircase with white risers opposite the door. The black man opened a door on the right-hand wall, and I went into a small sitting room that looked out over Thirty-seventh Street and the miniature garden. The walls were white-paneled, and there was a Tiffany lamp in green, red, and gold hanging in the center of the room. The rugs were Oriental, and the furniture was Edwardian.

The butler said, "Wait here, please," and left. He closed the door behind him.

There was a mahogany highboy on the wall opposite the windows with four cut-glass decanters and a collection of small crystal glasses. I took the stoppers out of the decanters and sniffed. Sherry, cognac, port, Calvados. I poured myself a glass of the Calvados. On the wall opposite the door was a black marble fireplace, and on either side floor-to-ceiling bookcases. I looked at the titles: *The Complete Works of Charles Dickens*, *A History of the English-Speaking Peoples* by Winston Churchill, *Longfellow: Complete Poetical and Prose Works*, H. G. Wells's *The Outline of History*, Chaucer's *The Canterbury Tales*, with illustrations by Rockwell Kent. The door opened behind me, and a woman entered. The butler closed it softly behind her.

"Mr. Spenser," she said, "I'm Patricia Utley," and put out her hand. I shook it. She looked as if she might have read all the books and understood them. She was fortyish, small and blond with good bones and big black-rimmed round glasses. Her hair was pulled back tight against her head with a bun in the back. She was wearing an off-white sleeveless linen dress with blue and green piping at the hem and along the neckline. Her legs were bare and tanned.

"Please sit down," she said. "I see you have a drink. Good. How may I help you?" I sat on the sofa. She sat opposite me on an ottoman. Her knees together, ankles crossed, hands folded in her lap.

"I'm looking for information about a girl named Donna Burlington who you probably knew about eight years ago." I showed her the picture.

"And why would you think I know anything about her, Mr. Spenser?"

"One of your colleagues suggested that she had left his employ and joined your firm."

"I'm sorry, I don't understand." Her blue eyes were direct and steady as she looked at me. Her face without lines.

"Well, ma'am, I don't mean to be coarse, but an East Village pimp named Violet told me she moved uptown and went to work for you in the late fall of nineteen sixty-six."

"I'm afraid I don't know anyone named Violet," she said.

"Tall, thin guy, aggressive dresser, but small-time. No reason for you to know him. The Pinkerton Agency has never heard of me either."

"Oh, I'm sure you're well known in your field, Mr. Spenser." She smiled, and a dimple appeared in each cheek. "But I really don't see how I can help you. This Violet person has misled you, I suppose for money. New York is a very grasping city."

The room was cool and silent, central air conditioning. I sipped the Calvados, and it reminded me that I hadn't eaten since about seven thirty. It was now almost four thirty. "Ms. Utley," I said, "I don't wish to rock your boat and I don't want anything bad to happen to Donna Burlington, I just need to know about her."

"Ms. Utley," she said. "That's charming, but it's Mrs., thank you."

"Okay, Mrs. Utley, but what I said stands. I need to know about Donna Burlington. Confidential. No harm to anyone, and I can't tell you why. But I need to know." I finished the brandy. She stood, took my glass, filled it, and set it down on the marble-topped coffee table in front of me. Her movements were precise and graceful and stylish. So was she.

"I have no quarrel with that, Mr. Spenser, but I can't help you. I don't know the young lady, nor can I imagine how anyone could think that I might."

"Mrs. Utley, I know we've only met, but

would you join me for dinner?"

"Is that part of your technique, Mr. Spenser? Candlelight and wine and perhaps I'll remember something about the young lady?"

"Well, there's that," I said. "But I hate to eat alone. The only people I know in the city are you and Violet, and Violet already had a date."

"Well, I don't know about being second choice to — what was it you said — an East Village pimp?"

"I'll tell you about my most exciting cases," I said. "Why, I remember one I call the howling dog caper . . ."

The dimple reappeared.

"And I'll do a one-hand push-up for you, and sing a dozen popular songs, pronouncing the lyrics so clearly that you can hear every word."

"And if I still refuse?"

"Then I go down to Foley Square and see if I can find someone in the DAs office that knows you and might put in a word for me."

"I do not like to be threatened, Mr. Spenser."

"Desperation," I said. "Loneliness and desire make a man crazy. Here, look at the kind of treat ahead of you." I put my glass on the end table, got down on the rug, and did a one-hand push-up. I looked up at her from the push-up position, my left hand behind my back. "Want to see another one?" I said.

She was laughing. Silently at first with her face serious but her stomach jiggling and giving her away, and then aloud, with her head back and the dimples big enough to hold a ripe olive.

"I'll go," she said. "Let me change, and we'll go. Now, for God sakes, get off the floor, you damn fool."

I got up. "The old one-hand push-up," I said. "Gets them almost every time."

She didn't take long. I had time to sip one more brandy before she reappeared in a backless white dress that tied around the neck and had a royal blue sash around the middle. Her shoes matched the sash, and so did her earrings.

I said, "Hubba, hubba."

"Hub-ba, hub-ba? What on earth does that mean?"

"You look very nice," I said. "Where would you like to go?"

"There's a lovely restaurant uptown a little ways we could try, if you'd like."

"I'm in your hands," I said. "This is your city."

"You are not, I would guess, ever in anyone's hands, Spenser, but I think you'll like this place."

"Cab?" I said.

"No, Steven will drive us."

When we went out the front door, there was the same well-built black man, sitting at the wheel of a Mercedes sedan. He'd swapped his mess jacket for a blue blazer.

We drove uptown.

The restaurant was at Sixty-fifth Street on the East Side and was called The Wings of the Dove.

"Do you suppose they serve the food in a golden bowl?" I said.

"I don't believe so. Why do you ask?"

"Henry James," I said. "It's a book joke."

"I guess I haven't read it."

It was only five thirty when we went in. Too early for most people to go to dinner, but most people had probably eaten lunch. I hadn't. It was a small restaurant, with a lavish dessert table in the foyer and two rooms separated by an archway. The ceiling was frosted glass that opened out, like a greenhouse, and the walls were used brick, some from the original building, some quite artfully integrated with the original. The tablecloths were pink, and there were flowers and green plants everywhere, many of them in hanging pots.

The maître d' in a tuxedo said, "Good evening, Mrs. Utley. We have your table."

She smiled and followed him. I followed her. One wall of the restaurant was mirrored, and it gave the illusion of a good deal more space than there was. I checked myself as we filed in. The suit was holding up, I'd had a haircut just last week, if only a talent scout from *Playgirl* spotted me.

"Would you care for cocktails?"

Patricia Utley said, "Compari on the rocks with a twist, please, John."

I said, "Do you have any draft beer?"

The maître d' said, "No."

I said, "Do you have any Amstel in bottles?"

He said, "No."

I said to Patricia Utley, "Is Nedick's still open?"

She said to the maître d', "Bring him a bottle of Heineken, John."

The maître d' said, "Certainly, Mrs. Utley," and stalked toward the kitchen.

She looked at me and shook her head slowly. "Are you ever serious, Spenser?"

"Yes, I am," I said. "I am serious, for instance, about discussing Donna Burlington with you."

"And I am serious when I say to you, why should you think I'd know her?"

"Because you are in charge of a high-priced prostitution operation and are bankrolled with what my source refers to as heavy money.

Now I know it, and you know it, and why not stop the pretense? The truth, Mrs. Utley, will set us free."

"All right," she said, "say you are correct. Why should I discuss it with you?"

A waiter brought our drinks and I waited while he put them down. Mine rather disdainfully, I thought.

"Because I can cause you aggravation — cops, newspapers, maybe the feds — maybe I could cause you trouble, I don't know. Depends on how heavy the bankrollers really are. If you talk with me, then it's confidential, there's no aggravation at all. And I might do another one-arm push-up for you."

"What if my bankrollers decided to cause you aggravation?"

"I have a very high aggravation tolerance."

She sipped her Campari. "It's funny, or maybe it's not funny at all, but you're the second person who's come asking about Donna."

"Who else?"

"He never said, but he was quite odd. He was, oh, what, in costume, I guess you'd say. Dressed all in white, white suit and shirt, white tie, white shoes and a big white straw hat like a South American planter."

"Tall and slim? Chewed gum?"

"Yes."

I said, "Aha."

"Aha?"

"Yeah, like Aha I see a connection, or Aha I have discovered a clue. It's detective talk."

"You know who he is then."

"Yes, I do. What did he want?"

She sipped some more Campari. I drank some Heineken. "Among my enterprises," she said, "is a film business. This gentleman had apparently seen Donna in one of our films and wanted the master print."

"Aha, aha!" I said. "Corporate diversification." The waiter came for our order. When he was gone, I said, "Start from the beginning. When did you meet Donna, what did she do for you, what kind of film was she in, tell me all."

"Very well, if you promise not to keep saying Aha."

"Agreed."

"Donna came to me through a client. He'd picked her up down in the East Village when he was drunk." She grimaced. "She was working for Violet then; her boyfriend had pimped for her before but had run from Violet. I don't know what happened to the boyfriend. The client thought she was too nice a girl to be hustling out of the back of a car with a two-dollar pimp like Violet. He put her in touch with me."

The waiter came with our soup. I had gazpacho; Patricia Utley had vichyssoise.

"I run a very first-rate operation, Spenser."

"I can tell that," I said.

"Of course, I would deny this to anyone if it ever came up."

"It won't. I don't care about your operation. I only care about Donna Burlington."

"But you disapprove."

"I don't approve or disapprove. To tell you the truth, Mrs. Utley, I don't give a damn. I think about one thing at a time. Right now I'm thinking about Donna Burlington."

"It's a volunteer business," she said. "It exists because men have needs." She said it as if the needs had a foul odor.

"Now who's disapproving?"

"You don't know," she said. "You've never seen what I've seen."

"About Donna Burlington," I said.

"She was eighteen when I took her. She didn't know anything. She didn't know how to dress, how to do her hair, how to wear makeup. She hadn't read anything, been anyplace, talked to anyone. I had her two years and taught her everything. How to walk, how to sit, how to talk with people. I gave her books to read, showed her how to make up, how to dress."

The waiter brought the fish. Sole in a saffron

sauce for her. Scallops St. Jacques for me.

"You and Rex Harrison," I said.

"Yes," she said. "It was rather like that. I liked Donna, she was a very unsophisticated little thing. It was like having a, oh not a daughter, but a niece perhaps. Then one day she left. To get married."

"Who'd she marry?"

"She wouldn't tell me — a client, I gathered, but she wouldn't say whom, and I never saw her again."

"When was this?"

Patricia Utley thought for a moment. "It was the same year as the Cambodian raids and the great protest, nineteen seventy. She left me in the winter of nineteen seventy. I remember it was winter because I watched her walk away in a lovely fur-collared tweed coat she had."

The waiter cleared the fish and put down the salad, spinach leaves with raw mushrooms in a lemon and oil dressing. I took a bite. So-so. "I assume the films were what I used to call dirty movies when I was a kid."

She smiled. "It is getting awfully hard to decide, isn't it? They were erotic films. But of good quality, sold by subscription."

"Black socks, garter belts, two girls and a guy? That kind of stuff?"

"No, as I said, tasteful, high quality, good

128

color and sound. No sadism, no homosexuality, no group sex."

"And Donna was in some?"

"She was in one, shortly before she left me. The pay was good, and while it was a lot of work, it was a bit of a change for her. Her film was called *Suburban Fancy*. She was quite believable in it."

"What did you tell the man who came asking?"

"I told him that he was under some kind of false impression. That I knew nothing about the films or the young lady involved. He became somewhat abusive, and I had to call for Steven to show him out."

"I heard this guy was pretty tough," I said.

"Steven was armed," she said.

"Oh," I said. "How come you didn't have Steven show me out?"

"You did not become abusive."

The entrée came. Duck in a fig and brandy sauce for me, striped bass in cucumber and crabmeat sauce for her. The duck was wonderful.

I said, "You sell these films by subscription." She nodded. "How's chances on a look at the subscription list?"

"None," she said.

"No chance?"

"No chance at all. Obviously you can see

my situation. Such material must remain confidential to protect our clients."

"People do sell mailing lists," I said.

"I do not," she said. "I have no need for money, Mr. Spenser."

"No, I guess you don't. Okay, how about I name a couple of people and you tell me if they're on your list? That doesn't compromise any but those I suspect anyway."

There were carrots in brown sauce with fresh dill and zucchini in butter with the entrée, and Patricia Utley ate some of each before she answered. "Perhaps we can go back to my home for brandy after dinner and I'll have someone check."

For dessert we had *clafoutis,* which still tastes like blueberry pancakes to me, and coffee. The coffee was weak. The bill was $119 including tip.

14

At Patricia Utley's home I returned to the Calvados. Patricia Utley had some sherry.

"Would you care to see the film, Spenser?" she said.

"No, thank you."

"Why not? I never met a man that didn't care for eroticism."

"Oh, I'm all for eroticism." I was thinking of Linda Rabb in her Church Park apartment in her clean white jeans. "It's movies I don't like."

"As you wish." She sipped some sherry. "You were going to mention some names to me."

"Yeah, Bucky Maynard — I don't know the real first name, maybe that's it — and Lester Floyd." I was gambling she'd never followed sports and had never heard of Maynard. I didn't want to tie Donna Burlington to the Red Sox, but I needed to know. If she'd ever heard of Bucky Maynard, she gave no sign. Lester didn't look like a self-starter. If he was in on this, it was a good bet he represented Maynard.

"I'll see," she said. She picked up a phone

131

on the end table near the couch and dialed a three-digit number. "Would you please check the subscription list, specifically on *Suburban Fancy,* and see if we have either a Bucky Maynard or a Lester Floyd, and the address and date? Thank you. Yes, call me right back, I'm in the library."

"How many copies of that film are there?" I asked.

"I won't tell you," she said. "That's confidential."

"Okay, it doesn't matter anyway. The real question is can I get all the copies?"

"No, I offered to show you the film and you didn't want to."

"That's not the point."

The phone rang and Patricia Utley answered, listened a moment, wrote on a note pad, and hung up.

"There is a Lester Floyd on our subscription list. There is no Bucky Maynard."

"What's the address on Floyd?"

"Harbor Towers, Atlantic Avenue, Boston, Mass. Do you need the street number?"

"No, thank you, that's fine." I finished my brandy and she poured me another.

"The point I was making before is that I don't want the films to look at. I want them to destroy. Donna Burlington has a nice life now. Married, kid, shiny oak floors in her living room, all-electric kitchen. Her husband loves her. That kind of stuff. These films could destroy her."

"That is hardly my problem, Spenser. The odds are very good that no one who saw these films would know Donna or connect her with them. And this is not eighteen seventy-five. Queen Victoria is dead. Aren't you being a little dramatic that someone who acted once in an erotic movie would be destroyed?"

"Not in her circles. In her circles it would be murder."

"Well, even if you are right, as I said, it is not my problem. I am in business, not social work. Destroying those films is not profitable."

"Even if purchased at what us collectors like to call fair market value?"

"Not the master. That would be like killing the goose. You can have all the prints you want, at fair market value, but not the master."

I got up and walked across the room and looked out the windows at Thirty-seventh Street. The streetlights had come on, and while it wasn't full dark yet, there was a softening bronze tinge to everything. The traffic was light, and the people who strolled by looked like extras in a Fred Astaire movie. Well dressed and good-looking. Brilliant red flowers the size of a trumpet bell bloomed in the little garden.

"Mrs. Utley," I said, "I think that Donna's being blackmailed and that the blackmailer will eventually ruin her life and her husband's and he's using your films."

Silence behind me. I turned around and put my hands in my hip pocket. "If I can get those films, I can take away his leverage." She sat quietly with her knees together and her ankles crossed as she had before and took a delicate sip of sherry. "You remember Donna, don't you? Like a niece almost. You taught her everything. Pygmalion. Remember her? She started out in life caught in a mudhole. And she's climbed out. She has gotten out of the bog and onto solid ground, and now she's getting dragged back in. You don't need money. You told me that."

"I'm a businesswoman," she said. "I do not follow bad business practices."

"Is that how you stay out of the bog?" I said.

"I beg your pardon?"

"You climbed out of the mudhole a bit too, is that how? You keep telling yourself you're a businesswoman and that's the code you live by. So that you don't have to deal with the fact that you are also a pimp. Like Violet."

There was no change in her expression.

"You lousy no-dick son of a bitch," she said.

I laughed. "Now, baby, now we are getting it together. You got a lot of style and great manners, but you and I are from the same neighborhood, darling, and now that we both know it maybe we can do business. I want those goddamned films, and I'll do what I have to to get them."

Her face was whiter now than it had been. I could see the makeup more clearly.

"You want her back in the mudhole?" I said. "She got out, and you helped her. Now she's got style and manners, and there's a man that wants to dirty her up and rub her nose in what she was. It'll destroy her. You want to destroy her? For business? When I said you were like Violet, you got mad. Think how mad it would make Violet." She reached over and picked up the phone and pressed the intercom button.

"Steven," she said, "I need you."

By the time the phone was back in the cradle, Steven was in the room. He had a nice springy step when he walked. Vigorous. He also had a .38 caliber Ruger Black Hawk.

Patricia Utley said, "I believe he has a gun, Steven."

Steven said, "Yeah, right hip, I spotted it when he came in. Shall I take it away from him?" Steven was holding the Ruger at his side, the barrel pointing at the floor. As he spoke, he slapped it absentmindedly against his thigh.

"No," Patricia Utley said, "just show him to the street, please."

Steven gestured with his head toward the door. "Move it," he said.

I looked at Patricia Utley. Her color had returned. She was poised, still controlled, handsome. I couldn't think of anything to say. So I moved it.

Outside, it was a warm summer night. Dark now, the bronze glow gone. And on the East Side, midtown, quiet. I walked over to Fifth Avenue and caught a cab uptown to my motel. The West Side was a little noisier but nowhere near as suave. When I got into my room, I turned up the air conditioner, turned on the television, and took a shower. When I came out, there was a Yankee game on and I lay on the bed and watched it.

Was it Lester? Was it Maynard with Lester as the straw? It had to be something like that. The coincidence would have been too big. The rumor that Rabb is shading games, the wife's past, Marty knew something about it. He lied about the marriage circumstances, and Lester Floyd showing up asking about the wife and Lester Floyd's name being on the mailing list. It had to be. Lester or Maynard had spotted

Linda Rabb in the film and put the screws on her husband. I couldn't prove it, but I didn't have to. I could report back to Erskine that it looked probable Rabb was in somebody's pocket and he could go to the DA and they could take it from there. I could get a print of the film and show Erskine and we could brace Rabb and talk about the integrity of the game and what he ought to do for the good of baseball and the kids of America. Then I could throw up.

I wasn't going to do any of those things, and I knew it when I started thinking about it. The Yankee game went into extra innings and was won by John Briggs in the tenth inning, when he singled Don Money in from third. Milwaukee was doing better in New York than I was.

15

I spent a good deal of time thinking about how to get the master print of *Suburban Fancy* from Patricia Utley and consequently spent not very much time sleeping till about 4:00 A.M. I didn't think of anything before I fell asleep, and when I woke up, it was almost 10 and I hadn't thought of anything while I slept. I was shaving at 10:20 when there was a knock at the door. I opened it with a towel around my middle, and there was a porter with a neat square package.

"Mr. Spenser?"

"Yeah."

"Gentleman asked me to give this to you."

I took it, went to the bureau, found two quarters, and gave them to the porter. He said thank you and went away. I closed the door and sat on the bed and opened the package. It was a canister of film. In the package was a note typed on white parchment paper.

Spenser,

This is the master print of *Suburban Fancy*. I have destroyed the remaining two copies in my possession. My records show a copy sold to the gentleman we discussed last night. There are ten other copies outstanding, but I can find no pattern in their distribution. You will have to deal with the gentleman mentioned above. I wish you success in that.

Doing this violates good business practice and has cost me a good deal more than the money involved. Violet would not have done it.

Yours,
Patricia C. Utley

She had signed it with a black felt-tipped pen in handwriting so neat it looked like type. I'd wasted a sleepless night.

I got out the Manhattan Yellow Pages from the bedside table and looked under "Photographic Equipment" till I found a store in my area that rented projectors. I was going to have to look at the film. If it turned out to be a film on traffic safety, or VD prevention, I would look like an awful goober. Patricia Utley had no reason particularly to lie to me but I was premising too much on the film's authenticity to proceed without looking.

I had mediocre eggs Benedict in the hotel coffee shop and went out and got my projector. Walking back up Fifty-seventh Street with it, I felt furtive, as if the watch and ward society had a tail on me. Going up in the elevator, I tried to look like an executive going to a sales conference. Back in my room I set up the projector on the luggage rack, pulled the drapes, shut off the lights, and sat on one of the beds to watch the movie. Wasteful practice giving me a room with two beds. Motels did that to me often. Alone in a two-bed room. A great song title, maybe I'd get me a funny suit and a guitar and record it. The projector whirred. The movie showed up on the bare wall.

Patricia Utley was right, it was a high-class operation. The color was good, even on the beige wall. I hadn't bothered with sound. The titles were professional, and the set was well lit and realistic-looking. The plot, as I got it without the sound, was about a housewife, frustrated by her church, children, and kitchen existence, who relieves her sense of limitation in the time-honored manner of skin flicks immemorial. The housewife was, in fact, Linda Rabb.

Watching in the darkened motel room, I felt nasty. A middle-aged man alone in a motel watching a dirty movie. When I got through here, I could go down to Forty-second Street and feed quarters into the peep show Movieolas. After the first sexual contact had established for sure what I was looking at, I shut off the projector and rewound the film. I went into the bathroom and stripped the film off the reel into the tub. I got the package of complimentary matches from the bedside table and lit the film. When it had burned up, I turned on the shower and washed the remnants down the drain. It was close to noon when I checked out of the hotel. Before I caught the shuttle back to Boston, I wanted to visit the Metropolitan Museum. On the way uptown in a cab, I stopped at a flower shop and had a dozen roses delivered to Patricia Utley. I checked my overnight bag at the museum, spent the afternoon walking about and throwing my head back and squinting at paintings, had lunch in the fountain room, took a cab to La Guardia, and caught the six o'clock shuttle to Boston. At seven forty-five I was home.

My apartment was as empty as it had been when I left, but stuffier. I opened all the windows, got a bottle of Amstel out of the refrigerator, and sat by the front window to drink it. After a while I got hungry and went to the kitchen. There was nothing to eat. I drank another beer and looked again, and found half a loaf of whole wheat bread behind the beer in the back of the refrigerator and an unopened jar of peanut butter in the cupboard. I made two peanut butter sandwiches and put them on a plate, opened another bottle of beer and went and sat by the window and looked out and ate the sandwiches and drank the beer. *Bas cuisine.*

At nine thirty I got into bed and read another chapter in Morison's *History* and went to sleep. I dreamed something strange about the colonists playing baseball with the British and I was playing third for the colonists and struck out with the bases loaded. In the morning I woke up depressed.

I hadn't worked out during my travels, and my body craved exercise. I jogged along the river and worked out in the BU gym. When I was through and showered and dressed, I didn't feel depressed anymore. So what's a strikeout? Ty Cobb must have struck out once in a while.

It was about ten when I went into the Yorktown Tavern. Already there were drinkers, sitting separate from each other smoking cigarettes, drinking a shot and a beer, watching *The Price Is Right* on TV or looking into the beer glass. In his booth in the back, Lennie Seltzer had set up for the day. He was reading the *Globe*. The *Herald American* and the New York *Daily News* were folded neatly on the table in front of him. A glass of beer stood by his right hand. He was wearing a light tan glen plaid three-piece suit today, and he smelled of bay rum.

He said, "How's business, kid?" as I slid in opposite him.

"The poor are always with us," I said. He started to gesture at the bartender, and I shook my head. "Not at ten in the morning, Len."

"Why not, tastes just as good then as any other time. Better, in fact, I think."

"That's what I'm afraid of. I got enough trouble staying sober now."

"It's pacing, kid, all pacing, ya know. I mean, I just sip a little beer and let it rest and sip a little more and let it rest and I do it all day and it don't bother me. I go home to my old lady, and I'm sober as a freakin' nun, ya know." He took an illustrative sip of beer and set the glass down precisely in the ring it had left on the tabletop. "Find out if Marty Rabb's going into el tanko yet?"

I shook my head. "I need some information on some betting habits, though."

"Uh-huh?"

"Guy named Lester Floyd. Ever hear of him?"

Seltzer shook his head. "How about Bucky Maynard?"

"The announcer?"

"Yeah. Floyd is his batman."

"His what?"

"Batman, like in the British army, each officer had a batman, a personal servant."

"You spend too much time reading, Spenser. You know more stuff that don't make you money than anybody I know."

" 'Tis better to know than not to know," I said.

"Aw bullshit, what is it you want to know about Maynard and what's'isname?"

"Lester Floyd. I want to know if they bet on baseball and, if they do, what games they bet on. I want the dates. And I need an idea of how much they're betting. Either one or both."

Seltzer nodded. "Okay, I'll let you know."

16

Lennie Seltzer called me two days later at my office. "Neither Maynard nor Floyd does any betting at all I can find out about," he said.

"Sonovabitch," I said.

"Screw up a theory?"

"Yeah. How sure are you?"

"Pretty sure. Can't be positive, but I been in business here a long time."

"Goddamn," I said.

"I hear that Maynard used to bet a lot, and he got into the hole with a guy and couldn't pay up and the guy sold the paper to a shylock. Pretty good deal, the guy said. Shylock gave him seventy cents on the dollar."

I said, "Aha."

Seltzer said, "Huh?"

I said, "Never mind, just thinking out loud. What's the shylock's name?"

"Wally Hogg. Real name's Walter Hogarth. Works for Frank Doerr."

"Short, fat person, smokes cigars?"

"Yeah, know him?"

"I've seen him around," I said. "Does he always work for Doerr, or does he free-lance?"

"I don't know of him free-lancing. I also don't know many guys like me ever made a profit talking about Frank Doerr."

"Yeah, I know, Lennie. Okay, thanks."

He hung up. I held the phone for a minute and looked up at the ceiling. Seventy cents on the dollar. That was a good rate. Doerr must have had some confidence in Maynard's ability to pay. I looked at my watch: 11:45. I was supposed to meet Brenda Loring in the Public Garden for a picnic lunch. Her treat. I put on my jacket, locked the office, and headed out.

She was already there when I arrived, sitting on the grass beside the swan boat pond with a big wicker basket beside her.

"A hamper?" I said. "A genuine wicker picnic hamper like in Abercrombie and Fitch?"

"I think you're supposed to admire me first," she said, "then the food basket. I've always been suspicious of your value system."

"You look good enough to eat," I said.

"I think I won't pursue that line," she said. She was wearing a pale blue linen suit and an enormous white straw hat. All the young executive types looked at her as they strolled by with their lunches hidden in attaché cases. "Tell me about your travels."

"I had a terrific blackberry pie in Illinois and a wonderful roast duck in New York."

"Oh, I'm glad for you. Did you also encounter any clues?" She opened the hamper as she talked and took out a red-and-white-checked tablecloth and spread it between us. The day was warm and still, and the cloth lay quiet on the ground.

"Yeah. I found out a lot of things and all of them are bad. I think. It's kind of complicated at the moment."

She took dark blue glossy-finish paper plates out of the hamper and set them out on the cloth. "Tell me about it. Maybe it'll help you sort out the complicated parts."

I was looking into the hamper. "Is that wine in there?" I said. She took my nose and turned my head away.

"Be patient," she said. "I went to a lot of trouble to arrange this and bring it out one item at a time and impress the hell out of you, and I'll not have it spoiled."

"Instinct," I said. "Remember I'm a trained sleuth."

"Tell me about your trip." She put out two sets of what looked like real silver.

"Okay, Rabb's got reason to be dumping a game or two."

"Oh, that's too bad."

"Yeah. Mrs. Rabb isn't who she's supposed to be. She's a kid from lower-middle America who smoked a little dope early and ran off

147

with a local hotshot when she was eighteen. She went to New York, was a whore for a while, and went into acting. Her acting was done with her clothes off in films distributed by mail. She started out turning tricks in one-night cheap hotels. Then she graduated to a high-class call girl operation run, or at least fronted, by a very swish woman out of a fancy town house on the East Side. That's when I think she met her husband."

Brenda placed two big wine goblets in front of us and handed me a bottle of rosé and a corkscrew. "You mean, he was a — what should I call him — a customer?"

"Yeah, I think so. How can I talk and open the wine at the same time? You know my powers of concentration."

"I've heard," she said, "that you can't walk and whistle at the same time. Just open the wine and then talk while I pour."

I opened the wine and handed it to her. "Now," I said, "where was I?"

"Oh, giant intellect," she said, and poured some wine into my glass. "You were saying that Marty Rabb had met his wife when she was — as we sociologists would put it — screwing him professionally."

"Words," I said, "what a magic web you weave with them. Yeah, that's what I think."

"How do you know?" She poured herself

a half glass of wine.

"Well, he's covering up her past. He lied about how he met her and where they were married. I don't know what he knows, but he knows something."

Brenda brought out an unsliced loaf of bread and took off the transparent wrapping.

"Sourdough?" I said.

She nodded and put the loaf on one of the paper plates. "Is there more?" she said.

"Yeah. A print of the film she made was sold to Lester Floyd." She looked puzzled. "Lester Floyd," I said, "is Bucky Maynard's gofer, and Bucky Maynard is, in case you forgot, the play by play man for the Sox."

"What's a gofer?"

"A lackey. Someone to go-for coffee and go-for cigarettes and go-for whatever he's told."

"And you think Maynard told him to go-for the film?"

"Yeah, maybe, anyway, say Bucky got a look at the film and recognized Mrs. Rabb. Is that smoked turkey?"

Brenda nodded and put a cranshaw melon out beside it, and four nectarines.

"Oh, I hope she doesn't know," she said.

"Yeah, but I think she does know. And I think Marty knows."

"Some kind of blackmail?"

"Yeah. First I thought it was maybe Maynard or Lester of the costumes getting Rabb to shave a game here and there and cleaning up from the bookies. But they don't seem to bet any these days, and I found out that Maynard owes money to a shylock."

"Is that like a loan shark?"

"Just like a loan shark," I said.

A large wedge of Monterey Jack cheese came out of the hamper, and a small crystal vase with a single red rose in it, which Brenda placed in the middle of the tablecloth.

"That hamper is like the clown car at the circus. I'm waiting for the sommelier to jump out with his gold key and ask if Monsieur is pleased with the wine."

"Eat," she said.

While I was breaking a chunk off the sourdough bread, Brenda said, "So what does the loan shark mean?"

I said, "Phnumph."

She said, "Don't talk with your mouth full. I'll wait till you've eaten a little and gotten control of yourself."

I drank some wine and said, "My compliments to the chef."

She said, "The chef is Bert Heidemann at Bert's Deli on Newbury Street. I'll tell him you were pleased."

"The shylock means that maybe Maynard

150

can't pay up and they've put the squeeze on him and he gave them Rabb."

"What do you mean, gave them Rabb?"

"Well, say Maynard owes a lot of bread to the shylock and he can't pay, and he can't pay the vig, and —"

"The what?"

"The vig, vigorish, interest. A good shylock can keep you paying interest the rest of your life and never dent the principal . . . like a revolving charge. . . . Anyway, say Maynard can't make the payments. Shylocks like Wally Hogg are quite scary. They threaten broken bones, or propane torches on the bottoms of feet, or maybe cut off a finger each time you miss a payment."

Brenda shivered and made a face.

"Yeah, I know, okay, say that's the case and along comes this piece of luck. Mrs. Rabb in the skin flick. He tells the shylock he can control the games that Marty Rabb pitches, and Rabb, being probably the best pitcher now active, if he's under control can make the shylock and his employers a good many tax-free muffins."

"But would he go for it?" Brenda asked. "I mean it would be embarrassing, but the sexual revolution has been won. No one, surely, would stone her to death."

"Maybe so if she were married to someone

in a different line of work, but baseball is more conservative than the entire city of Buffalo. And Rabb is part of a whole ethic: Man protects the family, no matter what."

"Even if he has to throw games? What about the jock ethic? You know winning isn't everything, it's the only thing. Wouldn't that be a problem?"

"That's not the real jock ethic, that's the jock ethic that people who don't know a hell of a lot about jocks believe. The real jock ethic's a lot more complicated."

"My, we're a little touchy about the jock ethic, aren't we?"

"I didn't mean you," I said.

"Maybe you haven't outgrown the jock ethic yourself."

"Maybe it's not something to outgrow," I said. "Anyway, some other time I'll give my widely acclaimed lecture on the real jock ethic. The thing is that unless I misjudged Rabb a lot, he's in an awful bind. Because his ethic is violated whichever way he turns. He feels commitment to play the game as best he can and to protect his wife and family as best he can. Both those commitments are probably absolute, and the point when they conflict must be sharp."

Brenda sipped some wine and looked at me without saying anything.

"A quarter for your thoughts if you accept Diners Club?"

She smiled. "You sound sort of caught up in all this. Maybe you're talking some about yourself too. I think maybe you are."

I leered at her. "Want me to tell you about the movie Mrs. Rabb was in and what they did?"

"You think I need pointers?" Brenda said.

"When we stop learning, we stop growing," I said.

"And you got us off that subject nicely, didn't you?"

I had once again qualified for membership in the clean plate club by then, and we had begun a second bottle of wine. "You have to get back to work?" I said.

"No, I took the afternoon off. I had the feeling lunch would stretch out."

"That's good," I said, and filled my wineglass again.

17

It was a classic summer morning when I dropped Brenda Loring off at her Charles River Park apartment. The river was a vigorous and optimistic blue, and the MDC cop at Leverett Circle was whistling "Buttons and Bows" as he directed traffic. Across the river Cambridge looked clean and bright in sharp relief against the sky. I went around Leverett Circle and headed back westbound on Storrow Drive. The last hurrah of the rush-hour traffic was still to be heard, and it took me twenty minutes to get to Church Park. I parked at a hydrant and took the elevator to the sixth floor. I'd called before I left that morning, so Linda Rabb was expecting me. Marty wasn't home; he was with the club in Oakland.

"Coffee, Mr. Spenser?" she said when I came in.

"Yeah, I'd love some," I said. It was already perked and on the coffee table with a plate of assorted muffins: corn, cranberry, and blueberry; all among my favorites. She was wearing pale blue jeans and a blue-and-pink-striped man-tailored shirt, open at the neck with a pink scarf knotted at the throat. On her feet were cork-soled blue suede slip-on shoes. The engagement ring on her right hand had a heart-shaped diamond in it big enough to make her arm weary. The wedding ring on her left was a wide gold band, unadorned. A small boy who looked like his father hung around the coffee table, eyeing the muffins but hesitant about snatching one from so close to me. I picked up the plate and offered him one, and he retreated quickly back behind his mother's leg.

"Marty's shy, Mr. Spenser," she said. And to the boy: "Do you want cranberry or blueberry, Marty?" The boy turned his head toward her leg and mumbled something I couldn't hear. He looked about three. Linda Rabb picked up a blueberry muffin and gave it to him. "Why don't you get your crayons," she said, "and bring them in here and draw here on the floor while I talk with Mr. Spenser?" The kid mumbled something again that I couldn't hear. Linda Rabb took a deep breath and said, "Okay, Marty, come on, I'll go with you to get them." And to me: "Excuse me, Mr. Spenser."

They went out, the kid hanging onto Linda Rabb's pants leg as they went. No wonder so many housewives ended up drinking Boone's Farm in the morning. They were back in maybe two minutes with a lined yellow legal-sized pad of paper and a box of crayons. The kid got down on the floor by his mother's chair and began to draw stick-figured people in various colors, with orange predominant.

"Now, what can I do for you, Mr. Spenser?" she asked.

I hadn't counted on the kid. "Well, it's kind of complicated, Mrs. Rabb, maybe I ought to come back when the boy isn't . . ." I left it hanging. I didn't know how much the kid would understand, and I didn't want him to think I didn't want him around.

"Oh, that's all right, Mr. Spenser, Marty's fine. He doesn't mind what we talk about."

"Well, I don't know, this is kind of ticklish."

"For heaven's sake, Mr. Spenser, say what's on your mind. Believe me, it is all right."

I drank some coffee. "Okay, I'll tell you two things; then you decide whether we should go on. First, I'm not a writer, I'm a private detective. Second, I've seen a film called *Suburban Fancy*."

She put her hand down on the boy's head; otherwise she didn't move. But her face got white and crowded.

"Who hired you?" she said.

"Erskine, but that doesn't matter. I won't hurt you."

"Why?" she said.

"Why did Erskine hire me? He wanted to find out if your husband was involved in fixing baseball games."

"O my God Jesus," she said, and the kid looked up at her. She smiled. "Oh, isn't that a nice family you're drawing. There's the momma and the daddy and the baby."

"Would it be better if I came back?" I said.

"There's nothing to come back for," Linda Rabb said. "I don't know anything about it. There's nothing to talk about."

"Mrs. Rabb, you know there is," I said. "You're panicky now and you don't know what to say, so you just say no, and hope if you keep saying it, it'll be true. But there's a lot to talk about."

"No."

"Yeah, there is. I can't help you if I don't know."

"Erskine didn't hire you to help us."

"I'm not sure if he did or not. I can always give him his money back."

"There's nothing to help. We don't need any help."

"Yeah, you do."

The kid tugged at his mother's pants leg again and held up his drawing. "That's lovely, Marty," she said. "Is that a doggie?" The kid turned and held the picture so I could see it.

I said, "I like that very much. Do you want

to tell me about it?"

The kid shook his head. "No," I said, "I don't blame you. I don't like to talk about my work all that much either."

"Marty," Linda Rabb said, "draw a house for the doggie." The boy bent back to the task. I noticed that he stuck his tongue out as he worked.

"Even if we did need help, what could you do?" Linda Rabb said.

"Depends on what exactly is going on. But this is my kind of work. I'm pretty sure to be better at it than you are."

My coffee cup was empty, and Linda Rabb got up and refilled it. I took a corn muffin, my third. I hoped she didn't notice.

"I've got to talk with Marty," she said.

I bit off one side of my corn muffin. Probably should have broken it first. Susan Silverman was always telling me about taking small bites and such. Linda Rabb didn't notice. She was looking at her watch. "Little Marty goes to nursery school for a couple of hours in the afternoon." She looked at the telephone and then at the kid and then at her watch again. Then she looked at me. "Why don't you come back a little after one?"

"Okay."

I got up and went to the door. Linda Rabb came with me. The kid came right behind her, close to her leg but no longer hanging on. As I left, I pointed my finger at him, from the hip, and brought my thumb down like the hammer of a pistol. He looked at me silently and made no response. On the other hand, he didn't run and hide. Always had a way with kids. The Dr. Spock of the gumshoes.

Outside on Mass Ave, I looked at my watch: 11:35. An hour and a half to kill. I went around the corner to the Y on Huntington Ave where I am a member and got in a full workout on the Universal, including an extra set of bench presses and two extra sets of wrist rolls. By the time I got showered and dressed my pulse rate was back down under 100 and my breathing was almost under control. At 1:15 I was back at Linda Rabb's door. She answered the first ring.

"Marty's at school, Mr. Spenser. We can talk openly," she said.

18

The coffee and muffins were gone. Linda Rabb said, "Has it been raining somewhere? Your hair's wet."

"Shower," I said. "I went over to the Y and worked out."

"Oh, how nice."

"Sound mind in a healthy body and all that."

"Could you show me some identification, Mr. Spenser?"

I got out the photostat of my license in its little plastic case and handed it to her. Also my driver's license. She looked at them both and gave them back.

"I guess you really are a detective."

"Thanks," I said, "I need reassurance sometimes."

"Just what do you know, Mr. Spenser?"

"I've been to Redford, Illinois, I've talked with Sheriff Donaldson and with your mother and father. I know you got busted there in 'sixty-six for possession of marijuana. I know you ran away with a guy named Tony Reece and that you haven't been back. I know you went to New York, that you lived in a rooming house on Thirteenth Street in the East Village,

160

that you were hustling for a living first for old Tony, then for a pimp named Violet. I know you moved uptown, went to work for Patricia Utley, made one pornographic movie, fell in love with one of your customers, and left to get married in the winter of nineteen seventy, wearing a lovely fur-collared tweed coat. I've been to New York, I've talked with Violet and with Patricia Utley, I preferred Mrs. Utley."

"Yes," Linda Rabb said without any expression, "I did too. Did you see me in the movie?"

"Yeah."

She was looking past me out the window. "Did you enjoy it?"

"I think you're very pretty."

She kept staring out the window. There wasn't anything to see except the dome of the Christian Science Mother Church. I was quiet.

"What do you want?" she said finally.

"I don't know yet. I told you what I know; now I'll tell you what I think. I think the client you married was Marty. I think someone got hold of *Suburban Fancy* that knows you and is blackmailing you and Marty, and that Marty is modifying some of the games he pitches so that whoever is blackmailing you can bet right and make a bundle."

Again silence and the stare. I thought about

moving in front of the window to intercept it.

"If I hadn't made the film," she said. "It was just a break, in a way, from turning tricks with strangers. I mean there was every kind of sex in it, but it was just acting. It was always just acting, but in the movie it was supposed to be acting and the guy was acting and there were people you knew around. You didn't have to go alone to a strange hotel room and make conversation with someone you didn't know and wonder if he might be freaky, you know? I mean, some of them are freaky. Christ, you don't know." She shifted her stare from the window to me. I wanted to look out the window.

"One film," she said. "One goddamned film for good money under first-class conditions and no S arid M or group sex, and right after that I met Marty."

"In New York?"

"Yes, they were in town to play the Yankees, and one of the other players set it up. Mrs. Utley sent three of us over to the hotel. It was Marty's first time with a whore." The word came out harsh and her stare was heavy on me. "He was always very straight."

More silence.

"He was a little drunk and laughing and making suggestive remarks, but as soon as we were alone, he got embarrassed. I had to lead him through it. And afterward we had some food sent up and ate a late supper and watched an old movie on TV. I still remember it. It was a Jimmy Stewart western called *Broken Arrow*. He kissed me good-bye when I left, and he was embarrassed to death to pay me."

"And you saw him again?"

"Yes, I called him at his hotel the next day. It was raining and the game with the Yankees was canceled. So we went to the Museum of Natural History."

"Yes."

"How about the other two players that night? Didn't they recognize you?"

"No, I had on a blond wig and different makeup. They didn't pay much attention to me anyway. Nobody looks at a whore. When I met Marty the next day, he didn't even recognize me at first."

"When did you get married?"

"When we said, except that we changed it. Marty and I worked out the story about me being from Arlington Heights and meeting in Chicago and all. I'd been to Chicago a couple of times and knew my way around okay if anyone wanted to ask about it. And Marty and I went out there before we were married and went to Comiskey Park, or whatever it's called now, and around Chicago so my story would sound okay."

"Where'd you get Arlington Heights?"

"Picked it out on a map."

We looked at each other. I could hear the faint hum of the refrigerator in the kitchen. And somewhere down the corridor a door opened and closed.

"That goddamned movie," she said. "When the letter came, I wanted to confess, but Marty wouldn't let me."

"What letter?"

"The first blackmail letter."

"Do you know who sent it?"

"No."

"I assume you don't have it."

"No."

"What did it say?"

"It said — I can remember it almost exactly — it was to Marty and it said, 'I have a copy of a movie called *Suburban Fancy*. If you don't lose your next ball game, I'll release it to the media.' "

"That's all?"

"That's all. No name or return address or anything."

"And did he?"

Linda Rabb looked blank. "Did he what?"

"Did Marty lose his next game?"

"Yes, he hung a curve in the seventh inning with the bases loaded against the Tigers, on purpose. I woke up in the middle of the night, that night, and he wasn't in bed, he was out in the living room, looking out the window and crying."

Her face was very white, and her eyes were puffy.

"And you wanted to confess it again."

"Yes. But he said no. And I said, 'It will kill you to throw games.' And he said a man looked out for his wife and his kid, and I said, 'But it will kill you.' And he wouldn't talk about it again. He said it was done and maybe there wouldn't be another letter, but we both knew there would."

"And there was."

She nodded.

"And they kept coming?"

She nodded.

"And Marty kept doing what they said to do?"

She nodded again.

"How often?" I said.

"The letters? Not often. Marty gets about thirty-five starts a year. There were maybe five or six letters last year, three so far this year."

"Smart," I said. "Didn't get greedy. Do you have any idea who it is?"

"No."

"It's a hell of a hustle," I said. "Blackmail

is dangerous if the victim knows you or at the point when the money is exchanged. This is perfect. There is no money exchanged. You render a service, and he gets the money elsewhere. He never has to reveal himself. There are probably one hundred thousand people who've seen that film, and you can't know who they are. He mails his instructions, bets his money, and who's to know?"

"Yes."

"And furthermore, the act of payment is itself a blackmailable offense so that the more you comply with his requests, the more he's got to blackmail you for."

"I know that too," she said. "If there was a hint of gambling influence, Marty would be out of baseball forever."

"If you look at it by itself, it's almost beautiful."

"I've never looked at it by itself."

"Yeah, I guess not." I said, "Is it killing Marty?"

"A little, I think. He says you get used to anything — maybe he's right."

"How are you?"

"It's not me that has to cheat at my job."

"It's you that has to feel guilty about it," I said. "He can say he's doing it for you. What do you say?"

Tears formed in her eyes and began to run

down her face. "I say it's what he gets for marrying a whore."

"See what I mean?" I said. "Wouldn't you rather be him?"

She didn't answer me. She sat still with her hands clenched in her lap, and the tears ran down her face without sound.

I got up and walked around the living room with my hands in my hip pockets. I'd found out what I was supposed to find out, and I'd earned the pay I'd hired on at.

"Did you call your husband?" I said.

She shook her head. "He's pitching today," she said, and her voice was steady but without inflection. "I don't like to bother him on the days he's pitching. I don't want to break his concentration. He should be thinking about the Oakland hitters."

"Mrs. Rabb, it's not a goddamned religion," I said. "He's not out there in Oakland building a temple to the Lord or a stairway to paradise. He's throwing a ball and the other guys are trying to hit it. Kids do it every day in school-yards all over the land."

"It's Marty's religion," she said. "It's what he does."

"How about you?"

"We're part of it too, me and the boy — the game and the family. It's all he cares about. That's why it's killing him because he has to screw us or screw the game. Which is like screwing himself."

I should be gone. I should be in Harold Erskine's office, laying it all out for him and getting a bonus and maybe a plaque: OFFICIAL MAJOR LEAGUE PRIVATE EYE. Gumshoe of the stars. But I knew I wasn't going to be gone. I knew that I was here, and I probably knew it back in Redford, Illinois, when I went to her house and met her mom and dad.

"I'm going to get you out of this," I said.

She didn't look at me.

"I know who's blackmailing you."

This time she looked.

19

I told her what I knew and what I thought.

"Maybe you can scare him off," she said. "Maybe when he realizes you know who he is, he'll stop."

"If he's wearing Frank Doerr's harness, I'd say no."

"Why?"

"Because he's got to be more scared of Frank Doerr than I can make him of me."

"Are you sure he's working for Frank What's'isname?"

"I'm not sure of anything. I'm guessing. Right after I started looking around the ball club, Doerr came to my office with one of his gunbearers and told me I might become an endangered species if I kept at it. That's suggestive, but it ain't definitive."

"Can you find out?"

"Maybe."

"Marty makes a lot of money. We could pay you. How much do you charge?"

"My normal retainer is two corn muffins and a black coffee. I bill the rest upon completion."

"I'm serious. We can pay a lot."

"Like Jack Webb would say, you already have, ma'am."

"Thank you."

"You're welcome."

"But I don't want you to start until we get Marty's approval."

"Un-unh. Your retainer doesn't buy that. I'm still also working for Erskine, and I'm still looking into the situation. I'm now looking with an eye to getting you unhooked, but you can't call me off."

"But you won't say anything about us?" Her eyes were wide and her face was pale and tight again and she was scared.

"No," I said.

"Not unless Marty says okay."

"Not until I've checked with you and Marty."

"That's not quite the same thing," she said.

"I know."

"But, Spenser, it's our life. It's us you're frigging around with."

"I know that too. I'll be as careful as I can be."

"Then, damn it, you have got to promise."

"No. I won't promise because I may not be able to deliver. Or maybe it will turn out different. Maybe I'll have to blow the whistle on you for reasons I can't see yet. But if I do, I'll tell you first."

"But you won't promise."

"I can't promise."

"Why not, goddamn you?"

"I already told you."

She shook her head once, as if there were a horsefly on it. "That's bullshit," she said. "I want a better reason than that for you to ruin us."

"I can't give you a better reason. I care about promises, and I don't want to make one I can't be sure I'll keep. It's important to me."

"Bullshit, bullshit, bullshit." She was leaning forward, and her nostrils seemed to flare wider as she did.

"My game has rules too, Mrs. Rabb."

"You sound like Marty," she said.

I didn't say anything.

She was looking at the Christian Science dome again. "Children," she said to it. "Goddamned adolescent children."

My stomach felt a little funny, and I was uncomfortable as hell.

"Mrs. Rabb," I said, "I will try to help. And I am good at this. I'll try."

She kept looking at the dome. "You and Marty and all the goddamned game-playing children. You're all good at all the games." She turned around and looked at me. "Screw," she said, and jerked her head at the door.

I couldn't think of much to say to that, so

I screwed. She slammed the door behind me, and I went down in the elevator feeling like a horse's ass and not sure why.

It was almost three o'clock. There was a public phone outside the drugstore next to the apartment building entrance. I went in and called Martin Quirk.

"Spenser," he said. "Thank God you called. I've got this murder took place in a locked room. It's got us all stumped and the chief said; 'Quirk,' he said, 'only one man can solve this.' "

"Can I buy you lunch or a drink or something?"

"Lunch? A drink? Christ, you must be in deep trouble."

I did not feel jolly. "Yes or no," I said. "If I wanted humor, I'd have called Dial-A-Joke."

"Yeah, okay. I'll meet you at the Red Coach on Stanhope Street."

I hung up. There was a parking ticket neatly tucked under the wiper blade on the driver's side. The string looped around the base. A conscientious meter maid. A lot of them just jam it under the wiper without looping the string, and sometimes on the passenger side where you can't even see it. It was nice to see samples of professional pride. I put the ticket in a public trash receptacle attached to a lamppost.

I drove down Boylston Street past the Prudential Center and the new public library wing and through Copley Square. The fountain in the square was in full spray, and college kids and construction workers mingled on the wall around it, eating lunch, drinking beer, taking the sun. A lot of them were shirtless. Beyond the fountain was the Copley Plaza with two enormous gilded lions flanking the entrance. And at the Clarendon Street end of the square, Trinity Church gleamed, recently sandblasted, its brown stones fresh-looking, its spires reflecting brightly in the windows of the Hancock Building. A quart of beer, I thought, and a cutlet sub. Shirt off, catch some rays, maybe strike up a conversation with a coed. Would you believe, my dear, I could be your father? Oh, you would.

I turned right on Clarendon and left onto Stanhope, where I parked in a loading zone. Stanhope Street is barely more than an alley and tucked into it between an electrical supply store and a garage is the Red Coach Grill, looking very old world with red tile roof and leaded windows. It was right back of police headquarters, and a lot of cops hung out there. Also a lot of insurance types and ad men. Despite that, it wasn't a bad place. Quiet lighting, oaken beams, and such. Quirk was at the bar. He looked like I always figured a cop ought to. Bigger than I am and thick. Short, thick black hair, thick hands and fingers, thick neck, thick features, a pockmarked face, and dressed like he'd just come from a summit meeting. Today he had on a light gray three-piece suit with a pale red plaid pattern, a white shirt, and a silk-finish wide red tie. His shoes were patent leather loafers with a gold trim. I slipped onto a barstool beside him.

"You gotta be on the take," I said. "Fuzz don't get paid enough to dress like that."

"They do if they don't do anything else. I haven't been on vacation in fifteen years. What are you spending your dough on?"

"Lunch for cops," I said. "Want to sit in a booth?"

Quirk picked up his drink, and we sat down across from the bar in one of the high-backed walnut booths that run parallel to the bar front to back and separate it from the dining room.

I ordered a bourbon on the rocks from the waitress. "Shot of bitters and a twist," I said, "and another for my date." The waitress was young with a short skirt and very short blond hair. Quirk and I watched her lean over the bar to pick up the drinks.

"You are a dirty lecherous old man," I said. "I may speak to the vice squad about you."

"What were you doing, looking for clues?"

"Just checking for concealed weapons, Lieutenant."

She brought the drinks. Quirk had Scotch and soda.

We drank. I took a lot of mine in the first swallow. Quirk said, "I thought you were a beer drinker."

"Yeah, but I got a bad taste I want to get rid of and the bourbon is quicker."

"You must be used to a bad taste in your line of business."

I finished the drink and nodded at the waitress. She looked at Quirk. He shook his head. "I'll nurse this," he said.

"I thought you guys weren't supposed to drink on duty," I said.

"That's right," he said. "What do you want?"

"I just thought maybe we could rap a little about law enforcement theory and prison reform, and swap detective techniques, stuff like that."

"Spenser, I got eighteen unsolved homicides in my left-hand desk drawer at this moment. You want to knock off the bullshit and get to it."

"Frank Doerr," I said. "I want to know about him."

"Why?"

"I think he owns some paper on a guy who

is squeezing a client."

"And the guy is squeezing the client because of the paper?"

"Yes."

"Doerr's probably free-lance. Got his own organization, operates around the fringe of the mob's territory. Gambling, mostly, used to be a gambler. Vegas, Reno, Cuba in the old days. Does loan sharking too. Successful, but I hear he's a little crazy, things don't go right, he gets bananas and starts shooting everybody. And he's too greedy. He's going to bite off too big a piece of somebody else's pie and the company will have him dusted. He's looking flashy now, but he's not going to last."

"Where do I find him?"

"If you're screwing around in this operation, he'll find you."

"But say I want to find him before he does, where?"

"I don't know, exactly. Runs a funeral parlor, somewhere in Charlestown. I get back to the station I'll check for you."

"Has he got a handle I can shake him with?"

"You? Scare him off? You try scaring Doerr and they'll be tying a tag on your big toe down at Boston City."

"Well, what's he like best? Women? Booze? Performing seals? There must be a way to him."

176

"Money," Quirk said. "He likes money. Far as I know he doesn't like anything else."

"How do you know he doesn't like me?" I said.

"I surmise it," Quirk said. "You met him?"

"Once."

"Who was with him?"

"Wally Hogg."

Quirk shook his head. "Get out of this, Spenser. You're in with people that will waste you like a popsicle on a warm day." The waitress brought us another round. She was wearing fishnet stockings. Could it be Ms. Right? I drank some bourbon.

"I wish I could get out of this, Marty. I can't."

"You're in trouble yourself?" Quirk asked.

"No, but I gotta do this, and it's not making anyone too happy."

"Wally Hogg," Quirk said, "will kill anyone Doerr tells him to. He doesn't like it or not like it. Slow or fast, one or a hundred, whatever. Doerr points him and he goes bang. He's a piece with feet."

"Well, if he goes bang at me," I said, "he'll be Wally Sausage."

"You're not as good as you think you are, Spenser. But neither is Captain Marvel. I've seen people worse than you, and maybe you got a chance. But sober. Don't go up against any of Doerr's group half-gassed. Go bright and early in the morning after eight hours' sleep and a good breakfast." He stirred the ice in his new drink. I noticed he hadn't finished the old one.

"Slow," I said. "Always knew you were a slow drinker." I reached over and picked up his old drink and finished it. "I can drink you right out of your orthopedic shoes, Quirk."

"Christ, this thing really is bugging you, isn't it?" Quirk said. He stood up. "I'm going back to work before you start to slobber."

"Quirk," I said.

He stopped and looked at me.

"Thanks for not asking for names."

"I knew you wouldn't tell me," Quirk said. "And watch your ass on this, Spenser. There must be someone who'd miss you."

I gave him a thumbs-up gesture, like in the old RAF movies, and he walked off. I drank Quirk's new drink and gestured to the waitress. There'll always be an England.

By five thirty in the afternoon I was sitting at the desk in my office, drinking bourbon from the bottle neck. Brenda Loring had a date, Susan Silverman didn't answer her phone. The afternoon sun slanted in at my window and made the room hot. I had the sash up, but there wasn't much breeze and the sweat was collecting where my back pressed against the chair.

Maybe I should get out of this thing. Maybe it bothered me too much. Why? I'd been told to screw before. Why did this time bother me? "Goddamned adolescent children." I'd heard worse than that before. "Goddamned game-playing children." I'd heard worse than that too. I drank some bourbon. My nose felt sort of numb and the surface of my face felt insulated. Dumb broad. Promises. Shit, I can't promise what I don't know. World ain't that simple, for crissake. I said I'd try. What the hell she want, for crissake? By God, I would get her out of it. I held the bottle up toward the window and looked at how much was left. Half. Good. Even if I finished it, there was another one in the file cabinet. Warm feeling having another one in the file cabinet. I winked at the file cabinet and grinned with one side of my mouth like Clark Gable used to. He never did it at file cabinets, though, far as I could remember. I drank some more and rinsed it around in my mouth. Maybe my teeth will get drunk. I giggled. Goddamned sure Clark Gable never giggled. Drink up, teeth. Hot damn. She was right, though, it was a kind of game. I mean, you played ball or something and whatever you did there had to be some kind of rules for it, for crissake. Otherwise you ended up getting bombed and winking at file cabinets. And your teeth got drunk. I giggled again. I was going to have Frank Doerr's ass. But sober, Quirk was right, sober, and in shape. "I'm coming, Doerr, you sonovabitch." Tongue wasn't drunk yet. I could still talk. Have a drink, tongue, baby. I drank. "Only where love and need are one," I said out loud. My voice sounded even stranger. Detached and over in the other corner of the room. "And the work is play for goddamned mortal stakes/Is the deed ever really done." My throat felt hot, and I inhaled a lot of air to cool it. "Mortal goddamned stakes," I said. "You got that, Linda Rabb/ Donna Burlington, baby?" I had unclipped my holster, and it lay with my .38 detective special in it on the desk beside the bourbon bottle. I drank a little more bourbon, put down the bottle, picked up the gun still in its holster, and pointed it at one of the Vermeer prints, the one of the Dutch girl with a milk pitcher. "How do you like them goddamned games, Frank?" Then I made a plonking sound with my tongue.

It was quiet then for a while. I sipped a little. And listened to the street sounds a little and then I heard someone snoring and it was me.

20

The next day it took me five miles of jogging and an hour and a half in the weight room to get the swelling out of my tongue and my vital signs functioning. I had breakfast in a diner, nothing could be finer, took two aspirin, and set out after Frank Doerr. A funeral parlor in Charlestown, Quirk had said. I brought all my sleuthing wiles to bear on the problem of how to locate it and looked in the Yellow Pages. Elementary, my dear Holmes. There it was, under "Funeral Directors": Francis X. Doerr, 228 Main Street, Charlestown. There's no escape Doerr.

With the top down I drove my eight-year-old Chevy across the bridge into City Square. Charlestown is a section of Boston. Bunker Hill is there, and *Old Ironsides,* but the dominant quality of Charlestown is the convergence of elevated transportation. The Mystic River Bridge, Route 93, and the Fitzgerald Expressway all interchange in Charlestown. Through the maze run the tracks of the elevated MBTA. Steel and concrete stanchions have flourished in the City Square area as nowhere else. If the British wanted to attack

Bunker Hill now, they wouldn't be able to find it.

From City Square I drove out Main Street under the elevated tracks. Doerr was maybe a half mile out from City Square toward Everett. Parking in that area of Charlestown was no problem. Most of the stores along that stretch of Main Street are boarded up. And urban renewal had not yet brought economic renewal. My car looked just right in the neighborhood.

Doerr's Funeral Parlor was a two-story brick house with a slate roof. It was wedged in between an unoccupied grocery store with plywood nailed over the windows and a discount shoe store called Ronny's Rejects. Across the street a vacant lot, not yet renewed, supported a flourishing crop of chicory and Queen Anne's lace. Nature never betrayed the heart that loved her.

I brushed my hand over the gun on my hip for security and rang the bell at the front door. Inside, it made a very gentle chime. Full of solicitude. The door was opened almost at once by a plump man with a perfectly bald head. Striped pants, white shirt, dark coat, black tie. The undertaker's undertaker.

"May I help you," he said. Soft. Solicitous. May I take your wallet, may I have all your money? Leave everything to us.

"Yes," I said. "I'd like to speak with Mr. Doerr." Mr. Doerr? He had me talking like him. I felt the scared feeling in my stomach.

"Concerning what, sir?"

I gave Baldy my card, the one with just my name on it, and said, "Tell Doerr I'd like to continue the discussion we began the other night." Dropping the "Mr." made me feel more aggressive.

"Certainly, sir, won't you sit down for a moment?"

I sat in a straight-back chair with a velvet seat, and the bald man left the room. I thought he might genuflect before he left but he didn't, just left with a dignified and reverent nod. It didn't help my stomach. Getting the hell out would have helped my stomach but would have done little for my self-image. Doerr probably wasn't that tough anyway. And Big Wally looked out of shape. Course you don't have to be in really great shape to squeeze off, say, two rounds from a nine-millimeter Walther.

The building was absolutely silent and had a churchy smell. The entry hall where I sat was papered in a dim beige with palm fronds on it. Very understated and elderly. The rug on the floor was Oriental, with dull maroon the dominant color, and the ceiling fixture was wreathed in molded plaster fruit.

The bald man came back. "This way, please, sir," he said, and stood aside to let me precede him through the door. Well, Spenser, I said, it's your funeral. Sometimes I'm uncontrollably droll.

Doerr's office was on the second floor front and looked out at the elevated tracks. Just right if you wanted to make eye contact with commuters. Apparently Doerr didn't because he sat behind a mahogany desk with his back to the window. His desk was cluttered with manila file folders. There were two phones, and a big vase of snapdragons flourished on a small stand beside the window.

"What do you want?" Doerr said.

I sat in one of the two straight chairs in front of the desk. Doerr didn't waste a lot of bread on decor.

"Why don't you get right to the point, Frank?" I said. "Don't hide behind evasive pleasantries."

"What do you want?"

"I want to answer some of the questions you asked me the other day."

"Why?"

"Openness and candor," I said. "The very hallmark of my profession."

Doerr was sitting straight, hands resting on the arms of his swivel chair. He looked at me without expression. Without comment. A train clattered by outside the window, headed for Sullivan Square. Doerr ignored it.

"Okay," I said. "You asked me what I was doing out at the ball park besides playing pepper."

Doerr continued to look at me.

"I was hired to see if someone was going into the tank out there."

Doerr said, "And?"

"And someone is."

"Who?"

"I think we both know."

"Why do you think that?"

"Several things, including the fact you came calling with your gunslinger right after I was out there."

"So?"

"So you heard from someone. I know who's dumping the games, I know who's blackmailing him into it, and I know what shylock the blackmailer owes. And that brings us right back here to you. Okay if I call you Shy for short? We get on so well and all."

"Names, Spenser. I'm not interested in a lot of bullshit about who you know and what anonymous whosis is doing what. Gimme a name and maybe I'm interested."

"Marty Rabb, Bucky Maynard, and you, Blue Eyes."

"Those are serious allegations, you got proof?"

"Serious allegations." I whistled. "That's very good for a guy whose lips move when he reads the funnies."

"Look, you piece of turd, don't get smart with me. I can have you blown away before you can scratch your ass. You understand? Now gimme what you got or you're going to get hurt."

"That's better," I said, "that's the old glib Frankie. Yeah, I got some proof, and I can get some more. What I haven't got for proof yet is the tie between you and Maynard, but I can get it. I'll bet Maynard might begin to ooze under pressure."

"Saying you're right, saying that's the way it is, and you can get some proof out of Maynard. Why don't I just waste Maynard or, maybe better, waste you?"

"You won't waste Maynard, because I'll bet you don't know what he's got on Rabb and I'll bet even more that he's got it stashed somewhere so if something happens to him, you'll never know. You won't waste me because I'm so goddamned lovable. And because there's a homicide cop named Quirk that knows I'm here. Besides, I'm not sure you got the manpower."

"You're doing a lot of guessing."

As far as you could tell from Doerr's face, I might have been in there arranging a low-budget funeral. And maybe I was.

"I'm licensed to," I said. "The state of Massachusetts says I'm permitted to make guesses and investigate them."

"So what do you want?"

"I want it to stop. I want Maynard to give me the item he's using for blackmail, and I want everyone to leave the Rabbs alone."

"Or what?"

"I don't suppose you'd accept 'or else.'"

"I'm getting sick of you, Spenser. I'm sick of the way you look, and the way you dress, and the way you get your hair cut, and the way you keep shoving your face into my work. I'm sick of you being alive and making wise remarks. You understand what I'm saying to you, turd?"

"What's wrong with the way I dress?"

"Shut up." Doerr's face had gotten a little red under the health club tan. He swung his chair sideways and stared out the window. And he had begun to fiddle with a pencil. Tapping it against his thigh until it had slid through his fingers and then reversing it and tapping it again. Tap-tap-tap. Reverse. Tap-tap-tap. Reverse. Lead end. Erasure end. Tap-tap-tap. Another train went by, almost empty, heading this time from Everett Station toward City Square. I slid my gun out of the hip holster and held it between my legs under my thighs with my hands clasped over it so it looked like I was leaning forward in concealed anxiety. I had no trouble at all simulating the anxiety.

Doerr swung his chair back around, still holding the pencil. He pointed it at me.

"Okay," he said. "I'm going to let you walk out of here. But before you go, I'm going to give you an idea of what happens when I get sick of someone."

There must have been a button under the desk that he could hit with his knee, or maybe the room was bugged. Either way a door to the left of the desk opened and Wally Hogg came in. He had on another flowered shirt, hanging outside the double knit pants, and the same wraparound sunglasses. In his right hand was one of those rubber truncheons that French cops use for riot control. He reminded me of one of the nasty trolls that used to lurk under bridges.

"Wally," Doerr said, looking at me while he said it, "show him what hurts."

Wally came around the desk. "You want it sitting down or standing up," he said. "It don't make no difference to me." He stood directly in front of me, looking down as I leaned over in even greater anxiety. I brought the gun up from between my thighs, thumbed the hammer back while I was doing that, and put the muzzle against the underside of his jaw, behind the jawbone, where it's soft. And I pressed up a little.

"Wally," I said, "have you ever thought of renting out as a goblin for Halloween parties?"

Wally's body was between Doerr and me, and Doerr couldn't see the gun. "What the hell are you waiting for, Wally? I want to hear him yelling."

I stood up and Wally inched back. The pressure of the gun muzzle made him rise slightly on the balls of his feet.

"Overconfidence," I said. "Overconfidence again, Frankie. That's twice you said ugly things to me and then couldn't back them up. Now I am thinking about whether I should shoot Wally in the tongue or not. Put the baton in my left hand, porklet," I said to Wally. He did. Our faces were about an inch apart, and his was as blank as it had been when he'd walked into the room. Without looking, I tossed it into the corner behind me.

"Of course, you could try me, Frank. You could rummage around in your desk maybe and come up with a weapon and have a go at me. Pretty good odds, Frankie. I have to shoot the Hog first before I can get you. Why not? It's quicker than scaring me to death."

I kept the pressure of the gun barrel up under Wally's chin and looked past his shoulder at Doerr. Doerr had his hands, palms down, on the desk in front of him. His face was quite red and his lips were trembling. But he didn't move. He stared at me and the lines from his nostrils to the corners of his mouth were deep and there was a very small tic in his left eyelid. With my left hand I patted Wally down and found the P .38 in its shoulder holster under his belt. All the time I watched Doerr. His mouth was open maybe an inch, and a small bubble of saliva had formed in the right-hand corner. I could see the tip of his tongue and it seemed to tremble, like the tic in his eye and in counterpoint to the movement of his lips. It was kind of interesting. But I was getting sick of standing that close to Wally.

"Turn around, Wall," I said. "Rest your hands on the desk and back away with your feet apart till all your weight is on your arms. You probably know the routine." I stepped away from him around the desk closer to Doerr, and Wally did as he was told.

"Okay, Frank," I said. "So much for what hurts. Are you going to climb down from Marty Rabb's back, or am I going to have to take you off?"

Doerr's mouth had opened wider and his tongue was quivering against his lower lip much more violently than it had been. The small bubble had popped and a small trickle of saliva had replaced it. His head had dropped, and as he began to look at me, he had to roll his eyes up toward his eyebrows. His mouth was moving too, but he wasn't making any noise.

"How about it, Frank? I like standing around watching you drool, but I got things to do."

Doerr opened his middle drawer and came out with a gun. I slammed my gun down on the back of his wrist, and it cracked against the edge of the desk. The gun rattled across the desk top and fell on the floor. Wally Hogg raised his head and I turned the gun at him. Doerr doubled up over his hand and made a repetitive grunting noise. Rocking back and forth in the swivel chair, grunting and drooling and making a sound that was very much like crying.

"Am I to interpret this as a rejection, Frank?"

He kept rocking and moaning and crying. "Aw balls," I said. I picked up Doerr's little automatic and stuck it in my pocket and said to Wally, "If you try to stop me, I'll kill you," and walked out the door. No one was downstairs. No one let me out. No one pursued me as I drove off.

21

There's a bird I read about that lives around rhinos and feeds on the insects that the rhinos stir up when they walk. I'd always figured that my work was like that. If the rhinos were moving, things would happen. This time, though, the rhino had started to cry and I wasn't too sure how to deal with that. I had a feeling, though, how Doerr would deal with that once he stopped crying. I didn't like the feeling. Maybe the technique only worked with real birds and real rhinos. Maybe I was doing more harm than good. Maybe I should get back on the cops and do what the watch commander said. I could get rid of a lot of maybes that way. I drove out Main Street, past the candy factory and around the circle at Sullivan Square, and back in toward Boston on Rutherford Ave. The sweet smell from the factory masked the smoke that billowed out of the skyscraper chimneys at the Edison plant across the Mystic River. Past the community college I turned right over the Prison Point Bridge, which had been torn down and rebuilt and called the Somebody T. Gilmore Bridge. The traffic reporters called it the Gilmore

Bridge, but I remembered when it led to the old prison in Charlestown, where the walls were red brick like the rest of the city, and on execution nights people used to gather in the streets to watch the lights dim when they turned on the current in the chair. Now state prison was in Walpole and electrocutions were accidental. Ah sweet bird of youth.

It was before lunchtime still and traffic was light. In five minutes I was at my office and sliding into a handy tow zone to park. I bought a copy of the *Globe* at a cigar store and went up to my office to read it. The Sox had an off day today and opened at home against Cleveland tomorrow. Marty Rabb had beaten Oakland 2 to 0 yesterday on the coast, and the team had flown into Logan this morning early.

I called Harold Erskine and got Bucky Maynard's home address. It was what I thought it would be.

"Why do you want to know?" Erskine asked.

"Because it's there," I said.

"I don't want you screwing around with Maynard. That's the surest way to have this whole thing blow wide open."

"Don't worry, I am a model of circumspection."

"Yeah," Erskine said, "sure. You find out anything yet?"

"Nothing I can report on yet, I need to put some things together."

"Well, for crissake, what have you found out? Is Marty or isn't he?"

"It's not that simple, Mr. Erskine. You'll have to give me a little more time."

"How much more? You're costing me a hundred a day. What do your expenses look like?"

"High," I said. "I been to Illinois and New York City and spent a hundred and nineteen bucks buying dinner for a witness."

"Jesus Galloping Christ, Spenser. I got a goddamned budget to work with, and I don't want you appearing in it. How the Christ am I going to bury that kind of dough? Goddamn it, I want you to check with me before you go spending my money like that."

"I don't work that way, Mr. Erskine, but I think I won't run up much more expense money." I needed to stay on this thing. I couldn't afford to get fired and shut off from the Sox. Also I needed the money. My charger needed feed and my armor needed polish. "I'm closing in on the truth."

"Yeah, well, close in on it quick," Erskine said, and hung up.

The old phrasemaker, Closing In on the Truth. I should have been a poet. If I went back on the cops, I wouldn't need to worry about charger feed and armor polish.

Harbor Towers is new, a complex of highrise apartments that looks out over Boston Bay. It represents a substantial monument to the renaissance of the waterfront, and the smell of new concrete still lingers in the lobbies. The central artery cuts them off from the rest of the city, penning them against the ocean, and they form a small peninsula of recent affluence where once the wharves rotted.

I parked in the permanent shade under the artery, on Atlantic Ave, near Maynard's apartment. It was hot enough for the asphalt to soften and the air conditioning in the lobby felt nice. I gave my name to the houseman, who called it up, then nodded at me. "Top floor, sir, number eight." The elevator was lined with mirrors and I was trying to see how I looked in profile when we got to the top floor and the doors opened. I looked quickly ahead, but no one was there. It's always embarrassing to get caught admiring yourself. Number 8 was opposite the elevator and Lester Floyd opened it on my first ring.

He had on white denim shorts, white sandals, a white headband, and sunglasses with big white plastic frames and black lenses. His upper body was as smooth and shiny as a snake's, tight-muscled and flexible. Instead of a belt, there was what looked like a black silk scarf passed through the belt loops and knotted over his left hip. He was chewing bubble gum. He held the door open and nodded his head toward the living room. I went in. He shut the door behind me. The living room looked to be thirty feet long, with the far wall a bank of glass that opened onto a balcony. Beyond the balcony, the Atlantic, blue and steady and more than my eye could fully register. Lester slid open one of the glass doors, went out, slid it shut behind him, settled down on a chaise made from filigreed white iron, rubbed some lotion on his chest, and chewed his gum at the sun. Mr. Warm.

I sat in a big red leather chair. The room was full of pictures, mostly eight-by-ten framed glossy prints of Maynard and various celebrities. Ballplayers, politicians, a couple of movie types. I didn't see any private eyes. Discriminatory bastard. Or maybe just discriminating. The sound of a portable radio drifted in faintly from Lester's sun deck. The top forty. Music with the enchantment and soul of a penny gum machine. Ah when you and I were young, Sarah.

Bucky Maynard came into the living room from a door in the far right-hand wall. He was wearing bright yellow pajamas under a maroon silk bathrobe with a big velvet belt. He needed a shave and his eyes were puffy.

He hadn't been awake long.

"Y'all keep some early hours, Spenser. Ah didn't get to bed till four A.M."

"Early to bed," I said, "early to rise. I wanted to ask you what Lester was doing down in New York talking with Patricia Utley."

The collar of Maynard's robe was turned up on one side. He smoothed it down carefully. "Ah can't say ah know what you mean, Spenser. Ah can ask him."

"As us kids say out in the bleachers, don't jive me, Bucko. Lester was down there on your business. I've talked with Utley. I've talked with Frank Doerr and Wally the bone breaker. I've seen a film called *Suburban Fancy* and I've talked with Linda Rabb. Actually I guess I asked the wrong question. I know what Lester was doing down there. What I want to know is what we do now that I know."

"Lester." Maynard showed no change in expression. Lester left the radio playing and came into the living room and blew a pink bubble that nearly obscured his face.

"Criminentlies, Lester," I said. "That's a really heavy bubble. I think you're my bubble-blowing idol. Zowie." Lester chewed the bubble back into his mouth without even a trace sticking to his lips. "Hours," I said. "It must take hours of practice."

Lester looked at Maynard. "Spenser and ah are going to talk, and ah want you to be around and to listen, Lester." Lester leaned against the edge of the sliding door and crossed his arms and looked at me. Maynard sat in one of the leather chairs and said, "Now what exactly is the point of your question, Spenser?"

"I figure that we've got a mutual problem and maybe we could conspire to solve it. Conspire, Lester. That means get together."

"Get to the point, Spenser. Lester gonna get mad at you."

"You owe Frank Doerr money and you can't pay, so you're blackmailing Marty Rabb into going into the tank for you and you're feeding the information to Doerr so he won't hurt you."

"Frank Doerr gotta deal with me before he hurts anybody," Lester said.

"Yeah, that's a big problem for him," I said. "Flex at him next time he and the Hog come calling. See if he faints."

"I'm getting goddamned sick of you, you wise bastard." Lester unfolded his arms and moved a step toward me.

"Lester," Maynard said, "we're talking." Lester refolded, stepped back, and leaned on the door again. Like reversing a film sequence.

"Ah don't know why you think all that stuff, Spenser. But say y'all was right. What business would that be of yours? You being a writer and all?"

"You know and I know that I'm not a writer."

"Ah do? Ah don't know any such thing. You told me you was a writer." The cornpone accent had gotten thicker. I didn't know if it was the real one coming through under duress or a fake one getting faker. Actually I couldn't see that it mattered much.

"Yeah, and you hollered to Doerr and he looked me up and we both know I'm a private cop."

"How about that?" Maynard raised both eyebrows. "A private detective. That still leaves the question, though, Spenser. What is your interest?"

"I would like you to stop blackmailing the Rabbs."

"And if ah was blackmailing them, and ah stopped, what would ah get out of that?"

"Well, I'd be grateful."

From his post by the sliding door, Lester said, "Shit," drawing it out into a two-syllable word.

"Anything besides that?" Maynard said.

"I'll help you with Frank Doerr."

Lester said, "Shit," again. This time in three syllables.

"Well, Spenser, that's awful kind of you,

199

but there's some things wrong with it all. One, ah don't much give a rat's ass for your gratitude, you know? And number two, ah don't figure, even if ah was having trouble with Frank Doerr, that you'd be the one ah'd ask to help me. And of course, number three, ah'm not blackmailing anybody. Am I, Lester?"

Lester shook his head no.

"So, ah guess you wasted some time coming up here. Interesting to know about you being a detective, though. Isn't that interesting, Lester?"

Lester nodded his head yes. From the radio on the sun deck the disk jockey was yelling about a "rock classic."

I said, "Y'all seem to be takin' the short view." Christ, now he had me doing it.

"Why do you say so?"

"Because you have only a short-term solution. How long will Marty Rabb pitch? Five more years. You think that when he's through with baseball, Doerr will be through with you? Doerr will feed on you till you die."

"I can handle Doerr," Lester said. He didn't get too much variety into the conversation.

"Lester," I said, "you can't handle Doerr. Handling Doerr is different from beating up some tourist in a bar or breaking bricks with your bare hand. Wally Hogg is a professional tough guy. You are an amateur. He would blow you away like a midsummer dandelion."

Lester said, "Shit." You find a line that works for you, I suppose you ought to stick with it.

Maynard said, "If these people are so tough, Spenser, what makes you think you can help?"

"Because I'm a professional too, Bucko, and that means I know what I can do and also what I can't do. It means I don't walk around thinking I can go up against the likes of Frank Doerr, head-on, without getting my body creased. It means I know how to even things up a bit. It means I know what I'm doing and you two clowns don't."

"You don't look so frigging tough to me," Lester said.

"That's the difference between you and me, Lester. Aside from our taste in music. I don't worry about how things look. You do. I don't have to prove whether I'm tough. You do. You'll say something like that to Wally the Hog and he'll shoot you three times or so in your nose, while you're posing and blowing bubbles."

Lester had gone into the stance, legs bent, left fist forward, right drawn back, clenched palms up, a little like the old pictures of the great John L. "Why don't you try me, you mother?"

I stood up. "Lester, let me show you something," I said. And brought my gun out and aimed it at his forehead. "This is a thirty-eight caliber Colt detective special. If I pull the trigger, your mastery of the martial arts will be of very little use to you."

Maynard said, "Now, Spenser . . ."

Lester looked at the gun.

"Now put that thing down, Spenser," Maynard said. "Lester. Y'all just relax over there."

Lester said, "If you didn't have that gun."

"But that's the point, Les, baby, I do have the gun. Wally Hogg has a gun. You don't have a gun. Professionals are the people with the guns who get them out first."

"Now relax, y'all, just relax," Maynard said.

"You won't always have that gun, Spenser."

"See, boy, see what a baby you are," I said. "You're wrong again. I will always have the gun. You'd forget the gun, you wouldn't have it where you could get at it, but I will always have it."

"Lester," Maynard said again. This time loud. "Y'all just settle down. You hear me. Now you settle down. Ah don't want no more of this."

Lester eased out of his attack stance and leaned back against the doorjamb, but he kept his eyes on me and one of the eyelids seemed to flicker as he stared. I put the gun away.

I said to Maynard, "You keep him away from me or I will hurt him badly."

"Now, Spenser," Maynard said. "Lester excites kind of prompt, but he's not a fool. Right, Lester?"

Lester didn't speak. I noticed that there was a glisten of sweat on Maynard's upper lip. "Suppose ah was interested in joining forces with you," Maynard said. "What would be your plan? How would you keep Doerr from coming around and killing me?"

"I'd tell him that right now we call off the scheme and end the blackmail and he's out some bread, but no one's incriminated. If he causes trouble, it'll mean the cops, and then someone will be incriminated. And it'll be him, because we've stashed evidence where the cops will find it if anything happens to you."

"What about the money I owe him, ah mean hypothetically?"

"You've paid that off long ago if Doerr got any bread down at all on Rabb's pitching."

"But maybe Doerr will want more, and ah don't have it."

"It'll be my job to convince him not to want more."

"That's it. That's the part ah want to know," Maynard said, and his face looked very moist. "How you going to convince him of anything?"

"I don't know. Appeal to his business sense. Dropping the scheme is a lot less trouble than sticking to it. He can pick up dough a lot of other ways. You and Rabb aren't the only goobers in the patch."

Maynard took a deep breath. The top forty played on outside on the deck. Lester glared at me from the doorjamb. Whitecaps continued to pattern the bay. Maynard shook his head. "Not good enough, Spenser. What you say may be so, but right now ah'm not getting hurt. And what you say makes getting hurt more likely."

"I can handle Doerr, Bucky." Lester sounded almost plaintive from the doorjamb.

"Maybe yes, maybe no, Lester. You couldn't have handled Spenser here, if it had been for real. Ah'm saying right now, no. Ah'm not going to take the chance. Things have worked out so far."

"But it's different now, Buck," I said. "I'm in it now. And I'm going to poke around and aggravate the hornets. It's not safe anymore to go along with the program."

"Maybe that's true too." Maynard said. "But ah got a choice between you and Frank Doerr, and right now ah'm betting on Frank Doerr. But ah'll tell you this. If you come up with something better than you have, ah'm willing to listen."

He had me. Maybe if I were he, I'd go that way too.

"Lester," Maynard said, "show Mr. Spenser out."

I shook my head. "I'll show myself out. I want Lester to stay there. Mad, like he is, he might slam the door on my foot."

Maynard nodded. There was a little drip of sweat at the tip of his beaky little canary nose. It was the last thing I saw as I backed out.

22

The Aquarium is near Harbor Towers, and I walked to it. Inside, it was nearly empty at midday, dark and cool and unconnected with the city outside. I went up the spiral walkway around it and watched the fish glide in silent pattern around and around the tank, swimming at different strata, sharks and groupers and turtles and fish I didn't know in the clear water. They were oblivious of me and seemed oblivious of each other as they swam in a kind of implacable order around and around the tank. The spiral walk was open and the rest of the aquarium was spacious. Below the flat pool, bottom lit and cool green, silhouetted other, smaller fish, black and quick in the bright water.

A small group of children, perhaps a second-grade class on a field trip, came in, shepherded by a plump little nun with horn-rimmed glasses. After a fast inspection of the fish, the children ignored them and began to enjoy the building and the space as if the real occasion for the visit was not the fish but the feel of the aquarium. The kids ran up and down the spiral and looked over the balcony and yelled at each other from above and below. The nun made no serious attempt to shush them, and the open space and the darkness seemed to absorb the noise. It was still nearly quiet.

I stood and stared in through the six-inch-thick glass windows of the tank and watched the sharks, small, well fed, and without threat, as they glided in their endless circle. I had screwed up the situation. I knew that. I had made Frank Doerr mad and Doerr was a cuckoo. Maynard was right not to buy what I was selling. Doerr wouldn't let Maynard off the hook and he wouldn't bargain with me. Maybe he never would have, but his honor was at stake now and he'd die before he let me talk him into, or scare him into, doing anything.

A small boy pushed in front of me to stare through the glass. His belt was too long, I noticed, and the surplus had been tucked through his belt loops halfway around his body. Another kid joined him and I found myself being moved away from the fish tank. Kids already know how to block out, I thought. I walked off the spiral and looked at the penguins on the first balcony. They were the false note in the place. There was no glass wall, no separation between us except six feet of space. The smell of fish and, I supposed, penguin was rank and uninsulated. I didn't like it. The silent fish in the lucid water were fantasy. The smelly penguins were real.

I went on back down the spiral and out into the bright hot day that met me with a clang as I came out of the aquarium. I could put Doerr and Maynard away by going to the cops. But that would humiliate Linda Rabb and probably get Marty Rabb barred from baseball. I could disarm Doerr and Maynard by getting Linda to make a public confession. But that would have the same results. The top was down on my car and the seats were hot and uncomfortable when I got in. I couldn't shake Maynard loose from Doerr. Doerr was the key and I had handled him wrong. If I got near him again, he'd try to kill me. It made negotiations difficult.

Back to the Rabbs. The lobby attendant called up, and Marty Rabb was waiting for me at the apartment door. His face was white, and the hinge muscles of his jaw were bunched.

"You sonovabitch," he said. His voice was hoarse.

"Maybe," I said, "but that won't help."

"What do you want now, plant a bug in our bedroom maybe?"

"I don't want to talk about it out in the corridor."

"I don't give a shit what you don't want.

208

I don't want you in my goddamned house, stinking up the place."

"Look, kid, I feel lousy and I understand how you feel, and I don't blame you, but I need to talk and I can't do it out here in the hall with you yelling at me."

"You're lucky I'm yelling, you bastard. You're lucky I don't knock you on your ass."

Linda Rabb came to the door beside her husband. "Let him in, Marty," she said. "We're in trouble. Yelling won't change that. Neither will hitting him."

"The sonovabitch caused it. We were doing all right till he came sticking his goddamned nose into things."

"I caused it as much as he did, Marty. I'm the whore, not Spenser."

Rabb turned at her. "I don't want to hear you say that again," he said. "Not again. I won't have any talk like that in my house. I don't want my son hearing that kind of talk."

Linda Rabb's voice sounded as if she were tired. "Your son's not home, Marty; he's at nursery. You know that. Come in, Spenser." She pulled Rabb away from the door, holding his right arm in both her hands. I went in.

I sat on the edge of the sofa. Rabb didn't sit. He stood looking at me with his hands clenched. "Be goddamned careful what you say, Spenser. I want to belt you so bad I can feel it in my guts, and if you make one smart remark, I'm going to level you."

"Marty, you are the third person this morning who has offered to disassemble my body. You are also third in order of probable success. I can't throw a baseball like you can, but the odds are very good that I could put you in the hospital before you ever got a hand on me." I was getting sick of people yelling at me.

"You think so."

I was proud of myself. I didn't say, "I know so."

Linda Rabb let go of his arm and came around in front of him and put both her arms around his waist. "Stop it, Marty. Both of you, grow up. This isn't a playground where you little boys can prove to each other how tough you are. This is our home and our future and little Marty and our life. You can't handle every problem as if it were an arm-wrestling contest." Her voice was getting thicker and she pressed her face against Rabb's chest. I knew she was crying, and I bet it wasn't the first time today.

"But, Jesus Christ, Linda, a man's gotta —"

She screamed at him, the voice muffled against his chest. "Shut up. Just shut up about a man's gotta."

I wished I smoked. It would have given me something to do with my hands. Rabb put his arms around his wife and rubbed the top of her head with his chin.

"I don't know," he said. "I don't know what in hell to do."

"Me either," I said. "But if you'd sit down, maybe we could figure something out."

Linda Rabb said, "Sit down, Marty," and pushed him away from her with both hands against his chest. He sat. She sat beside him, her head turned away, and wiped her eyes with a Kleenex.

"I don't know," Rabb said again. He was sitting on the edge of the couch, his elbows on his thighs, his hands clasped together between his knees, staring at his thumbnails. Then he looked up at me.

"How much does Erskine know?" he said.

"Nothing. He had heard just the hint that something might not be square. He hired me to prove it was square. He wants to believe it's square and you're square."

"Yeah," Rabb said, "I'm square okay. You got any good ideas?"

"Your wife's told you what I said yesterday?" He nodded. "I've talked with Doerr and I've talked with Maynard. Doerr won't let go of Maynard and Maynard won't let go of you. He's too scared."

"Maynard really is in debt to a loan shark?"
"Yes."

"I can't see anything else to do but keep on the way we have been," Rabb said.

"If you can stand it," I said.

"You can stand what you can't change," Rabb said. "You got a better idea?"

"You could blow the whistle."

Linda Rabb had finished with her Kleenex and was looking at us again.

"Yes," she said.

"No," Rabb said.

"Marty," she said.

"No."

"Marty," she said again, "we can't stand it. I can't stand it. I can't stand the guilt and watching how you feel every time you lose a game so they can make money."

"I don't always have to lose," he said. "Sometimes I give up a run or two for the inning pools."

"Don't quibble, Marty. You're in a funk for a week after every letter. You have lived too long believing in do-or-die for dear old Siwash. It's killing you and it's killing me."

"I'm not having your name blabbed all over the country. You want your kid to hear that kind of talk about his mother? Maybe we should show him the movie."

"It will pass, Marty. He's only three."

"And it'll make nice talk in the bullpen, you know. You want me to listen to those bastards laughing in the dugout when I go out to pitch? Or maybe that doesn't matter either because if it gets out that I been dumping games I won't be pitching anyway. You want that?"

"No, but I don't want this either, Marty."

"Yeah, well maybe you should have thought of that when you were spreading your legs in New York."

I felt a jangle of shock in my solar plexus. Linda Rabb never flinched. She looked at her husband steadily. The silence hung between them. It was Rabb who broke it. "Jesus, honey, I'm sorry," he said and put his arms around her. She didn't pull away, but her body was as stiff and remote as a wire coat hanger and her eyes were focused on something far beyond the room as he held her.

"Jesus," he said again, "Jesus Christ, what is going to happen to us? What are we going to do?"

23

"What would you do if you didn't play ball?" I said.

"Coach."

"And if you didn't coach?"

"Scout, maybe."

"And if you couldn't scout and couldn't coach? If you were out of baseball altogether?"

Rabb was looking at his thumbnails again. "I don't know," he said.

"What did you major in in college?"

"Phys ed."

"Well, what would you like to do?"

"Play ball and then coach."

"I mean, if you couldn't play ball." Rabb stared harder at his thumbnails. Linda Rabb looked at the coffee table. Neither one spoke.

"Mrs. Rabb?"

She shook her head.

"How sure are you that if this all comes out you'll be suspended?" I said to Rabb.

"Sure," he said. "I threw some games. If the commissioner's office finds out, I'm finished for life."

"What if I confessed," Linda Rabb said. "If I told everyone about my past and no one said anything about the gambling part. I could say Marty didn't even know about me."

"They could still blackmail me with the fact I dumped the games," Rabb said.

"Not necessarily," I said. "If I could find a way to get Doerr out of it, we might be able to bargain with Maynard. If Maynard told about you, he'd have to tell about himself. He'd be out of work too. With Maynard you'd have a standoff."

"Doesn't matter," Rabb said. He looked up from his thumbnails. "I won't let her." Linda Rabb was looking at me too.

"Could you get Doerr out of it, Spenser?"

"I don't know, Mrs. Rabb. If I can't, we're stuck. I guess I'll have to."

"She's not saying anything about it. What the hell kind of a man do you think I am?"

"How can you?" Linda Rabb said, and I realized we weren't paying attention to Marty.

"I don't know," I said.

"If you can, I'll do it," she said.

"No," Rabb said.

"Marty, if he can arrange it, I'll do it. It's for me too. I can't stand watching you pulled apart like this. You love two things, us and baseball, and you have to hurt one to help the other. I can't stand knowing that it's my fault, and I can't stand the tension and the fear and the uncertainty. If Spenser can do

215

something about the other man, I will confess and we'll be free."

Rabb looked at me. "I'm warning you, Spenser."

"Grow up, Marty," I said. "The world's not all that clean. You do what you can, not what you oughta. You're involved in stuff that gets people dead. If you can get out of it with some snickers in the bullpen and some embarrassment for your wife, you call that good. You don't call it perfect. You call it better than it was."

Rabb was shaking his head. Linda Rabb was still looking at me. She nodded. I noticed that her body was still stiff and angular, but there was color in her face. Rabb said, "I . . ." and shook his head again.

I said, "We don't need to argue now. Let me see what I can do about Doerr. Maybe I can't do anything about him. Maybe he'll do something about me. But I'll take a look."

"Don't do anything without checking here," Rabb said.

I nodded. Linda Rabb got up and opened the door for me. I got up and walked out. No one said be careful, or win this one for the Gipper, or it counts not if you win or lose but how you play the game. In fact, no one said anything, and all I heard as I left was the door closing behind me.

Outside on Mass Ave I looked at my watch: 1:30. I went home.

In my kitchen I opened a can of beer. I was having trouble getting Amstel these days and was drinking domestic stuff. Didn't make a hell of a lot of difference, though. The worst beer I ever had was wonderful. The apartment was very quiet. The hum of the air conditioner made it seem quieter. Doerr was the key. If I could take him out of this, I could reason with Maynard. All I had to do was figure out what to do about Doerr. I finished the beer. I didn't know what to do about Doerr. I applied one of Spenser's Rules: When in doubt, cook something and eat it. I took off my shirt, opened another can of beer, and studied the refrigerator.

Spareribs. Yeah. I doused them with Liquid Smoke and put them in the oven. Low. I had eaten once in a restaurant in Minneapolis, Charlie's something-or-other, and had barbecued spareribs with Charlie's own sauce. Since then I'd been trying to duplicate it. I didn't have it right yet, but I'd been getting close. This time I tried starting with chili sauce instead of ketchup. What did Doerr like? I'd been through that: money. What was he afraid of? Pain? Maybe. He hadn't liked me whacking his hand. I put a little less brown sugar in with the chili sauce this time. But maybe he hadn't liked me standing up to him. He was a weird guy and his reaction might be more complicated than just crying because his hand hurt. Two cloves of garlic this time. But first another beer, helps neutralize the garlic fumes. Either way I had got to him today. So what? I squeezed a couple of lemons and added the juice to my sauce. The smell of the spareribs was beginning to fill the kitchen. Even with the air conditioner on, the oven made the kitchen warm and sweat trickled down my bare chest.

Getting to Doerr and getting him to do what I wanted were different things. I had a feeling that right now if I saw him, I'd have to kill him. I never met a guy before who actually foamed at the mouth. If I killed, I'd have to kill the Hog. Maybe a little red wine. I hadn't tried that before. I put in about half a cupful. Or would I? If Doerr were dead, the Hog might wither away like an uprooted weed. Best if I never found out. One dash of Tabasco? Why not? I opened another beer. If I were dead, I'd shrivel up like an uprooted weed. I put the sauce on to cook and began to consider what else to have. Maybe I could call Wally and Frank over and cook at them until they agreed to terms. Way to a man's heart and all that.

There was zucchini squash in the vegetable

drawer, and I sliced it up and shook it in flour and set it aside while I made a beer batter. It always hurt me to pour beer into a bowl of flour, but the results were good. That's me. Mr. Results. Lemme see, what was I going to do about Frankie Doerr? The barbecue sauce began to bubble, and I turned the gas down to simmer. I put two dashes of Tabasco into the beer batter and stirred it and put it aside so the yeast in the beer would work on the flour.

I looked in the freezer. Last Sunday Susan Silverman and I had made bread all afternoon at her house while we watched the ball game and drank Rhine wine. She had mixed and I had kneaded and at the end of the day we had twelve loaves, baked and wrapped in foil. I'd brought home six that night and put them in the freezer. There were four left. I took one out and put it in the oven, still in the foil. Maybe old Suze would have an idea about what to do with Frankie Doerr, or how to get my barbecue sauce to taste like Charlie's or whether I was drinking too much lately. I looked at my watch: 3:30. She'd be home from school. I called her and let it ring ten times and she didn't answer, so I hung up. Brenda Loring? No. I wanted to talk about things I had trouble talking about. Brenda was for fun and wisecracks and she did a terrific picnic, but she wasn't much better than I was at talking about hard things.

The spareribs were done and the bread was hot. I dipped my sliced zucchini in the beer batter and fried it in a little olive oil. I'd eaten alone before. Why didn't I like it better this time?

24

I ate and drank and thought about my problem for the rest of the afternoon and went to bed early and woke up early. When I woke up, I knew what I was going to do. I didn't know how yet, but I knew what.

It was drizzly rainy along the Charles. I ran along the esplanade with my mind on other things, and it took a lot longer to do my three miles. It always does if you don't concentrate. I was on the curb by Arlington Street, looking to dash across Storrow Drive and head home, when a black Ford with a little antenna on the roof pulled alongside and Frank Belson stuck his head out the window on the passenger side and said, "Get in."

I got in the back seat and we pulled away. "Drive around for a while, Billy," Belson said to the other cop, and we headed west toward Allston.

Belson was leaning forward, trying to light a cigar butt with the lighter from the dashboard. When he got it going, he shifted around, put his left arm on the back of the front seat, and looked at me.

"I got a snitch tells me that Frank Doerr's

going to blow you up."

"Frank personally?"

"That's what the snitch says. Says you roughed Frank up yesterday and he took it personally." Belson was thin, with tight skin and a dark beard shaved close. "Marty thought you oughta know."

We stayed left where the river curved and drove out Soldiers Field Road, past the 'BZ radio tower.

"I thought Wally Hogg did that kind of work for Doerr."

"He does," Belson said. "But this one he's gonna do himself."

"If he can," I said.

"That ain't to say he might not have Wally around to hold you still," Belson said.

Billy U-turned over the safety island and headed back in toward town. He was young and stylish with a thick blond mustache and a haircut that hid his ears. Belson's sideburns were trimmed at the temple.

"Reliable snitch?"

Belson nodded. "Always solid in the past."

"How much you pay him for this stuff?"

"C-note," Belson said.

"I'm flattered," I said.

Belson shrugged. "Company money," he said.

We were passing Harvard Stadium. "You

or Quirk got any thoughts about what I should do next?"

Belson shook his head.

"How about hiding?" Billy said. "Doerr will probably die in the next ten, twenty years."

"You think he's that tough?"

Billy shrugged. Belson said, "It's not tough so much. It's crazy. Doerr's crazy. Things don't work out, he wants to kill everybody. I hear he cut one guy up with a machete. I mean, cut him up. Dis-goddamn-membered him. Crazy."

"You don't think a dozen roses and a note of apology would do it, huh?"

Billy snorted. Belson didn't bother. We passed the Kenmore exit.

I said to Billy, "You know where I live?" He nodded.

Belson said, "You got a piece on you?"

"Not when I'm running," I said.

"Then don't run," Belson said. "If I was Doerr, I coulda aced you right there at the curb when we picked you up."

I remembered my lecture to Lester about professionals. I had no comment. We swung off at Arlington and then right on Marlborough. Billy pulled up in front of my apartment.

"You're going up a one-way street," I said to Billy.

"Geez, I hope there's no cops around," Billy said.

I got out. "Thanks," I said to Belson.

He got out too. "I'll walk up to your place with you."

"With me? Frank, you old softy."

"Quirk told me to get you inside safe. After that you're on your own. We don't run a babysitting service. Not even for you, baby."

When I unlocked my apartment door, I noticed that Belson unbuttoned his coat. We went in. I looked around. The place was empty. Belson buttoned his coat.

"Watch your ass," he said and left.

From my front window I looked down while Belson got in the car and Billy U-turned and drove off. Now I knew what and was getting an idea of how. I took my gun from the bureau drawer and checked the load and brought it with me to the bathroom. I put it on the toilet seat while I took a shower and put it on the bed while I dressed. Then I stuck the holster in my hip pocket and clipped it to my belt. I was wearing broken-in jeans and white sneakers with a racing stripe and my black polo shirt with a beaver on the left breast. I wasn't up in the alligator bracket yet. I put on a seersucker jacket, my aviator sunglasses, and checked myself in the hall mirror. Battle dress.

I unlocked the front hall closet and got out a 12-gauge Iver Johnson pump gun and a box of double-aught shells. Then I went out. In the hall I put the shotgun down and closed a toothpick between the jamb and the hinge side of the door, a couple of inches up from the ground. I snapped it off so only the edge was visible at the crack of the door. It would be good to know if someone had gone in.

I picked up the shotgun and went out to my car. On the way down I passed another tenant. "Hunting season so early?" he said.

"Yeah."

Outside I locked the shotgun and the box of shells in the trunk of my car, got in, put the top down, and headed for the North Shore. I knew what and how, now I had to find where.

I drove Route 93 out of Boston through Somerville and Medford. Along the Mystic River across from Wellington Circle, reeds and head-high marsh grass still grew in an atmosphere made garish with neon and thick exhaust fumes. Past Medford Square, I turned off 93 and took the Lynn Fells Parkway east, looking at the woods and not seeing what I was looking for. Medford gave way to Melrose. I turned off the Fellsway and drove up around Spot Pond, past the MDC Zoo in Stoneham, and back into Melrose. Still nothing that looked right to me. I drove through Melrose, past red clay tennis courts by the lake, past the high school and the Christian Science Church. Just before I got to Route 1, I turned off into Breakhart Reservation. Past the MDC skating rink the road narrows to a single lane and becomes one way. I'd been there on a picnic once with Susan Silverman, and I knew that the road looped through the woods and returned here, one way all the way. There were saddle trails, and lakes, and picnic areas scattered through thick woods.

Thirty yards into the reservation I found the place. I pulled off the narrow hot top road, the bushes scraping my car fenders and crunching under the tires, and got out. A small hill sloped up from the road, and scooped out of the side of it was a hollow the size of a basketball court and the shape of a free-form pool. About in the middle was a flat-planed granite slab, higher than a man's head at one end that tapered into the ground in a shape vaguely like a shark fin.

The sides of the gully were yellow clay, streaked with erosion troughs, scattered with small white pines. The sides sloped steeply up to the somewhat gentler slope of the hill, which was thick with white pine and clustered birch saplings and bunches of sumac. I walked into the hollow and stood by the slab of granite. The high end was a foot above my head. There was a high hum of locust in the hot, still woods and the sound of birds. A squirrel shot down the trunk of a birch tree and up the trunk of a maple without pausing. I took my coat off and draped it over the rock. Then I scrambled up the slope of the gully and looked down. I walked around the rim of the hollow, looking at the woods and at the sun and down into the hollow. It would do. I looked at my watch: 2:00.

I went back down, put my coat on again, got in my car, and drove on around the loop and out of the reservation. There was a small shopping center next to the exit road and I parked my car in among a batch of others in front of a Purity Supreme Supermarket. There was a pay phone in the supermarket, and I used it to call Frank Doerr.

He wasn't in, but the solicitous soft-voiced guy that answered said he'd take a message.

"Okay," I said, "my name is Spenser. S-p-e-n-s-e-r, like the English poet. You know who I am?"

"Yeah, I know." No more solicitude.

"Tell Frank if he wants to talk to me, he should drive up to the Breakhart Reservation in Saugus. Come in by the skating rink entrance, drive thirty yards down the road. Park and walk into the little gully that's there. He'll know it. There's a big rock like a shark fin in the middle of the gully. You got that?"

"Yeah, but why should he want to see you? Frank wants to see someone he calls them into the office. He don't go riding around in the freaking woods."

"He'll ride around in them this time because if he doesn't, I am going to sing songs to the police that Frank will hate the sound of."

"If Frank does want to do this, and I ain't saying he will, when should he be there?"

"Six o'clock tonight."

"For crissake, what if he ain't around at that time? Maybe he's busy. Who the Christ you think you're talking to?"

"Six o'clock tonight," I said, "or I'll be down on Berkeley Street crooning to the fuzz." I hung up.

25

I bought a pound of Hebrew National bologna, a loaf of pumpernickel, a jar of brown mustard, and a half gallon of milk and walked back to my car. I opened the trunk and got an old duffel bag from it. I put the shotgun, the shells, and my groceries in the duffel bag, closed the trunk, shouldered the duffel bag, and walked back toward Breakhart.

It took about fifteen minutes for me to walk back to my gully in the hillside. I climbed up the hill past it, halfway to the top of the hill, and found a thick stand of white pine screened by some dogberry bushes that let me look down into the hollow and the road below it. I took my groceries, my shotgun, and my ammunition out of the duffel bag, took off my coat, and put it in the duffel bag. I spread the bag on the ground, sat down on it, and loaded the shotgun. It took six shells. I put six extras in my hip pocket and cocked the shotgun and leaned it against the tree. Then I got out my groceries and made lunch. I spread the mustard on the bread with my pocketknife and used the folded paper bag as a plate. I drank the milk from the carton. Not bad. Nothing like dining al fresco. I looked at my watch: 2:45. I ate another sandwich. Three o'clock. The locusts keened at me. Some sparrows fluttered above me in the pines. On the road below cars with children and mothers and dogs and inflatable beach toys drove slowly by every few minutes but less often as the afternoon wore on.

I finished the milk with my fourth sandwich and wrapped the rest of the bread and bologna back up in the paper sack and shoved it in the duffel bag. At four fifteen a silver gray Lincoln Continental pulled off the road by the gully and parked for a long time. Then the door opened and Wally Hogg climbed out. He was alone. He stood and looked carefully all over the hollow and up the hill at where I sat behind my bushes and everywhere else. Finally he looked up and down the road, reached back into the car, and came out with a shoulder weapon. He held it inconspicuously down along his leg and stepped away from the car and in behind the trees along the road. The Lincoln started up and drove away.

In the shelter of the trees Wally was less careful with the weapon, and I got a good look at it. An M-16 rifle. Standard U.S. infantry weapon. 7.62 millimeter. Twenty rounds. Fancy carry handle like the old BARs and a pistol grip back of the trigger housing like the old Thompsons. M-16? Christ, I was just getting used to the M-1.

Wally and his M-16 climbed the gully wall about opposite me. He was wearing stacked-heel shoes. He slipped once on the steep sides and slid almost all the way back down. Hah! I made it first try. When the Lincoln had arrived, I'd picked up the shotgun and held it across my lap. I noticed that my hands were a little sweaty as I held it. I looked at my knuckles. They were white. Wally didn't climb as high as I had. Too fat. Ought to jog mornings, Wally, get in shape. A few yards above the gully edge he found some thick bushes and settled in behind them. From the hollow he would be invisible. Once he got settled, he didn't move and looked like a big toad squatting in his ambush.

I looked at my watch again. Quarter of five. Some people went by on horseback, the shod hooves of the horses clattering on the paved road. It was a sound you didn't hear often, yet it brought back the times when I was small and the milkman had a horse, and so did the trash people. And manure in the street, and the sparrows. All three of the horses on the road below were a shiny, sweat-darkened chestnut color. The riders were kids. Two girls in white blouses and riding boots, a boy in jeans and no shirt.

231

The draft horses that used to pull the trash wagons were much different. Big splayed feet and massive, almost sumptuous haunches. Necks that curved in a stolid, muscular arch. When I was very small, I remembered, horses pulling a scoop were used to dig a cellar hole on the lot next to my house.

The riders disappeared and the clopping dwindled. Wally Hogg still sat there, silent and shapeless, watching the road. I heard a match scrape and smelled cigarette smoke. Careless Wally, what if I were just arriving and smelled the smoke? It carries out here in the woods. But Wally probably wasn't all that at home in the woods. Places Wally hung out you could probably smoke a length of garden hose and no one would smell it. The woods were dry, and I hoped he was careful with the cigarette. I didn't want this thing getting screwed up by a natural disaster.

I checked my watch again: 5:15. My chest felt tight, as if the diaphragm were rusty, and I had that old tingling toothache feeling in behind my navel. There was a lump in my throat. Above me the sky was still bright blue in the early summer evening, dappling through the green leaves. Five thirty, getting on toward supper. The road was empty now below me. The mommas and the kids and the dogs were going home to get supper going and eat with

Daddy. Maybe a cookout. Too hot to eat in tonight. Maybe a couple of beers and some gin and tonic with a mint leaf in the glass. And after supper maybe the long quiet arc of the water from the hoses of men in shirt sleeves watering their lawns. My stomach rolled. Smooth. How come Gary Cooper's stomach never rolled? Oh, to be torn 'tween love and duty, what if I lose . . . Five forty. My fingertips tingled and the nerves along the insides of my arms tingled. The pectoral muscles, particularly near the outside of my chest, up by the shoulder, felt tight, and I flexed them, trying to loosen up. I took two pieces of gum out of my shirt pocket and peeled off the wrappers and folded the gum into my mouth. I rolled the wrappers up tight and put them in my shirt pocket and chewed on the gum. Quarter of six. I remembered in Korea, before we went in at Inchon, they'd fed us steak and eggs, not bologna and bread, but it hadn't mattered. My stomach rolled before Inchon too. And at Inchon I hadn't been alone. Ten of six.

I looked down at Wally Hogg. He hadn't moved. His throat wasn't almost closed, and he wasn't taking deep breaths and not getting enough oxygen. He thought he was going to sit up there and shoot me in the back when Frank Doerr gave the nod, which would be

233

right after Frank Doerr found out exactly what I had on him and if I'd given anything to the cops. Or maybe Doerr wanted to fan me himself and Wally was just backup. Anyway, we'd find out pretty soon, wouldn't we? Seven of six. Christ, doesn't time flit by when you're having a big time and all?

I stood up. The shotgun was cocked and ready. I carried it muzzle down along my leg in my right hand and began to move down the hill in a half circle away from where Wally Hogg was. I was about 100 yards away. If I was careful, he wouldn't hear me. I was careful. It took me ten minutes to get down the slope to the road, maybe 50 yards down the road beyond the gully.

Still daylight and bright, but under the trees along the road a bit dimmer than midday. I stayed out of sight behind some trees just off the road and listened. At five past six I heard a car stop and a door open and close. With the shotgun still swinging along by my side, I walked up the road toward the dell. High-ho a dairy-o. The car was a maroon Coupe de Ville, pulled off on the shoulder of the road. No one was in it. I went past it and turned into the hollow. The sun was shining behind me and the hollow was bright and hot. Doerr was standing by the shark-fin rock. Maroon slacks, white shoes, white belt, black shirt, white tie, white safari jacket, black-rimmed sunglasses, white golf cap. A really neat dresser. Probably a real slick dancer too. His hands were empty as I walked in toward him. I didn't look up toward Wally. But I knew where he was, maybe thirty yards up and to my left. I kept the rock on his side of me as I walked into the gully. I kept the shotgun barrel toward the ground. Relaxed, casual. Just had it with me and thought I'd bring it along. Ten feet from Doerr, with the shark-fin rock not yet between me and Wally Hogg, I stopped. If I got behind the rock, Wally would move.

"What the hell is the shotgun for, Spenser?" Doerr said.

"Protection," I said. "You know how it is out in the woods. You might run into a rampaging squirrel or something."

I could feel Wally Hogg's presence up there to my left, thirty yards away. I could feel it along the rib cage and in my armpits and behind the knees. He wasn't moving around. I could hear him if he did; he wasn't that agile and he wasn't dressed for it. You can't sneak around in high-heeled shoes unless you take them off. I listened very hard and didn't hear him.

"I hear you have been bad-mouthing me, Frankie."

"What do you mean?"

"I mean you been saying you were going to blow me up."

Still no sound from Wally. I was about five feet from the shelter of the rock.

"Who told you that?"

I wished I hadn't thought about Wally taking his shoes off.

"Never mind who told me that. Say it ain't so, Frankie."

"Look, shit-for-brains. I didn't come out here into the freakin' woods to talk shit with a shit-for-brains like you. You got something to say to me or not?"

"You haven't got the balls, Frankie."

Doerr's face was red. "To blow you up? A shit-for-brains pimple like you? I'll blow you up anytime I goddamned feel like it."

"You had the chance yesterday in your office, Frankie, and I took your piece away from you and made you cry."

Doerr's voice was getting hoarse. The level of it dropped. "You got me out here to talk shit at me or you got something to say?"

I was listening with all I had for Wally. So hard I could barely hear what Doerr was saying.

"I got you out here to tell you that you're a gutless, slobbering freak that couldn't handle an aggressive camp fire girl without hiring someone to help you." I was splitting my concentration, looking at Doerr as hard as I was listening for Wally, and the strain made the sweat run down my face. I almost grunted with the effort.

Doerr's voice was so hoarse and constricted he could barely talk. "Don't you dare talk to me that way," he said. And the oddly quaint phrase squeezed out like dust through a clogged filter.

"You gonna cry again, Frankie? What is it? Did your momma toilet-train you funny? Is that why you're such a goddamned freak-o?"

Doerr's face was scarlet and the carotid arteries stood out in his neck. His mouth moved, but nothing came out. Then he went for his gun. I knew he would sometime.

I brought the pump up level and shot him. The gun flew from his hand and clattered against the shark-fin rock and Doerr went over backwards. I didn't see him land; I dove for the rock and heard Wally's first burst of fire spatter the ground behind me. I landed on my right shoulder, rolled over and up on my feet. Wally's second burst hit the rock and sang off in several directions. I brought the shotgun down over the slope end of the rock where it was about shoulder-high and fanned five rounds into the woods in Wally Hogg's area as fast as I could pump.

I was back down behind the rock, feeding my extra rounds into the magazine, when I heard him fall. I looked and he came rolling through the brush down the side of the gully and came to a stop at the bottom, face up, the front of him already wet with blood. Leaves and twigs and dirt had stuck to the wetness as he rolled. I looked at Doerr. At ten feet the shotgun charge had taken most of his middle. I looked away. A thick and sour fluid rose in my throat and I choked it down. They were both dead. That's the thing about a shotgun. At close range you don't have to go around checking pulses after.

I sat down and leaned back against the rock. I hadn't planned to, and I didn't want someone to find me there. But I sat down anyway because I had to. My legs had gotten weak. I was taking deep breaths, yet I didn't seem to be getting enough oxygen. My body was soaking wet and in the early evening I was feeling cold. I shivered. The sour fluid came back and this time I couldn't keep it down. I threw up with my head between my knees and the two stiffs paying no attention.

Beautiful.

26

It was quarter to seven. I had the shotgun back in the duffel bag and the duffel bag back in the trunk of my car and my car on the overpass where the Fellsway meets Route 1. I drove north on 1 toward Smithfield. On the way I stopped and bought a quart of Wild Turkey bourbon. Turning off Route 1 toward Smithfield Center, I twisted the top off, took a mouthful, rinsed my mouth, spit out the window, and drank about four ounces from the bottle. My stomach jumped when the booze hit it, but then it steadied and held. I was coming back. I drove past the old common, with its white church and meetinghouse, and turned left down Main Street. I'd been up here a year or so back on a case and since then had learned my way around the town pretty well. At least I knew the way to Susan Silverman's house. She lived 100 yards up from the common in a small weathered shingle Cape with blue window boxes filled with red petunias. Her car was in the driveway. She was home. It hadn't occurred to me until now that she might not be.

I walked up the brick path to her front door.

On either side of the path were strawberry plants, white blossoms, green fruit, and some occasional flashes of ripe red. A sprinkler arced slowly back and forth. The front door was open and I could hear music which sounded very much like Stan Kenton. "Artistry in Rhythm." Goddamn.

I rang her bell and leaned against the doorjamb, holding my bottle of Wild Turkey by the neck and letting it hang against my thigh. I was very tired. She came to the door. Every time I saw her I felt the same click in my solar plexus I'd felt the first time I saw her. This time was no different. She had on faded Levi cutoffs and a dark blue ribbed halter top. She was wearing octagonal horn-rimmed glasses and carried a book in her right hand, her forefinger keeping the place.

I said, "What are you reading?"

She said, "Erikson's biography of Gandhi."

I said, "I've always liked Leif's work."

She looked at the bourbon bottle, four ounces gone, and opened the door. I went in.

"You don't look good," she said.

"You guidance types don't miss a trick, do you?"

"Would it help if I kissed you?"

"Yeah, but not yet. I been throwing up. I need a shower. Then maybe we could sit down and talk and I'll drink the Wild Turkey."

"You know where," she said. I put the bourbon down on the coffee table in the living room and headed down the little hall to the bathroom. In the linen closet beside the bathroom was a shaving kit of mine with a toothbrush and other necessaries. I got it out and went into the bathroom. I brushed and showered and rinsed my mouth under the shower and soaped and scrubbed and shampooed and lathered and rinsed and washed for about a half an hour. Out, out, damned spot.

When I got through, I toweled off and put on some tennis shorts I'd left there and went looking for Susan. The stereo was off, and she was on the back porch with my Wild Turkey, a bucket of ice, a glass, a sliced lemon, and a bottle of bitters.

I sat in a blue wicker armchair and took a long pull from the neck of the bottle.

"Were you bitten by a snake?" Susan said.

I shook my head. Beyond the screen porch the land sloped down in rough terraces to a stream. On the terraces were shade plants. Coleus, patient Lucy, ajuga, and a lot of vincas. Beyond the stream were trees that thickened into woods.

"Would you like something to eat?"

I shook my head again. "No," I said. "Thank you."

"Drinking bourbon instead of beer, and declining a snack. It's bad, isn't it?"

I nodded. "I think so," I said.

"Would you like to talk about it?"

"Yeah," I said, "but I don't quite know what to say."

I put some ice in the glass, added bitters and a squeeze of lemon, and filled the glass with bourbon. "You better drink a little," I said. "I'll be easier to take if you're a little drunk too."

She nodded her head. "Yes, I was thinking that," she said. "I'll get another glass." She did, and I made her a drink. In front of the house some kids were playing street hockey and their voices drifted back faintly. Birds still sang here and there in the woods, but it was beginning to get dark and the songs were fewer.

"How long ago did you get divorced?" I asked.

"Five years."

"Was it bad?"

"Yes."

"Is it bad now?"

"No. I don't think about it too much now. I don't feel bad about myself anymore. And I don't miss him at all anymore. You have some part in all of that."

"Mr. Fixit," I said. My drink was gone and I made another.

"How does someone who ingests as much as you do get those muscle ridges in his stomach?" Susan said.

"God chose to make me beautiful instead of good," I said.

"How many sit-ups do you do a week?"

"Around a zillion," I said. I stretched my legs out in front of me and slid lower in the chair. It had gotten dark outside and some fireflies showed in the evening. The kids out front had gone in, and all I could hear was the sound of the stream and very faintly the sound of traffic on 128.

"There is a knife blade in the grass," I said. "And a tiger lies just outside the fire."

"My God, Spenser, that's bathetic. Either tell me about what hurts or don't. But for crissake, don't sit here and quote bad verse at me."

"Oh damn," I said. "I was just going to swing into *Hamlet*."

"You do and I'll call the cops."

"Okay," I said. "You're right. But bathetic? That's hard, Suze."

She made herself another drink. We drank. There was no light on the porch, just that which spilled out from the kitchen.

"I killed two guys earlier this evening," I said.

"Have you ever done that before?"

"Yeah," I said. "But I set these guys up."

"You mean you murdered them?"

"No, not exactly. Or . . . I don't know. Maybe."

She was quiet. Her face a pale blur in the semidarkness. She was sitting on the edge of a chaise opposite me. Her knees crossed, her chin on her fist, her elbow on her knee. I drank more bourbon.

"Spenser," she said, "I have known you for only a year or so. But I have known you very intensely. You are a good man. You are perhaps the best man I've ever known. If you killed two men, you did it because it had to be done. I know you. I believe that."

I put my drink on the floor and got up from the chair and stood over her. She raised her face toward me and I put one hand on each side of it and bent over and looked at her close. She had a very strong face, dark and intelligent, full of kinetic suggestion, with faint laugh lines at the corners of her mouth. She was still wearing her glasses, and her big dark eyes looked bigger through the lenses.

"Jesus Christ," I said.

She put her hands over mine and we stayed that way for a long time.

Finally she said, "Sit."

I sat and she leaned back on the chaise and pulled me down beside her and put my head against her breast. "Would you like to make love?" she said.

I was breathing in big low inhales. "No," I said. "Not now, let's just lie here and be still."

Her right arm was around me and she reached up and patted my cheek with her left hand. The stream murmured and after a while I fell asleep.

27

It was a hot, windy Tuesday when I finished breakfast with Susan and drove back into Boston. I stopped on the way to look at the papers. The *Herald American* had it, page one, below the fold: GANGLAND FIGURE GUNNED DOWN. Doerr and Wally Hogg had been found after midnight by two kids who'd slipped in there to neck. State and MDC police had no comment as yet.

Under the expressway, street grit was blowing about in the postcommuter lull as I pulled up and parked in front of Harbor Towers. I went through the routine with the houseman again and went up in the elevator. Bucky Maynard let me in. He was informal in a Boston Red Sox T-shirt stretched over his belly.

"What do you want, Spenser?" Informal didn't mean friendly. Lester leaned against the wall by the patio doors with his arms folded across his bare chest. He was wearing dark blue sweat pants and light blue track shoes with dark blue stripes. He blew a huge pink bubble and glared at me around it.

"It's hard to look tough blowing bubbles,

Lester," I said. "You ever think about a pacifier?"

"Ah asked what you want, Spenser." Maynard still had his hand on the door.

I handed him the paper. "Below the fold," I said, "right side."

He looked at it, read the lead paragraph, and handed it to Lester.

"So?"

"So, maybe your troubles are over."

"Maybe they are," Maynard said.

"So are Marty Rabb's troubles over too?"

"Troubles?"

"Yeah, maybe you'll stop sucking on him now that Frank Doerr's not going to suck on you anymore."

"Spenser, y'all aren't making any sense. Ah'm not doing anything to Marty Rabb. Ah don't know, for a fact, what you are talking of."

"You're going to recoup your losses," I said. "You mean, stupid sonovabitch."

"No reason to stand there shaking your head, Spenser. Ah'm the one should be offended."

"Doerr bled Rabb through you, and you never got any blood. Now he's dead, you want yours."

"Ah think you ought to leave now, Spenser. You're becoming abusive."

Lester popped his bubble gum and tittered. There were newspapers on the coffee table, the *Globe* and the *Herald American*. They'd known before I got here, and Maynard had already figured out that he had the money machine now.

"Don't you want to know why I think you're stupid?" I said.

"No, ah don't."

"Because you were off the hook, clean. And you won't take the break."

"Move out," Lester said. "And just keep in mind, Spenser, if anybody was blackmailing Rabb, they could get him for throwing games just as much as for marrying a whore."

"Never mind, Lester," Maynard said sharply. "We don't know anything about it and Spenser is on his way out."

"I'd be glad to make him go faster, Buck."

"He's on his way, Lester. Aren't you, Spenser?"

"Yeah, I am, but as they say in all the movies, Bucky, I'll be back."

"Ah wouldn't if ah were you. Ah can't restrain Lester too much more."

"Well, do what you can," I said. "I don't want to kill him." Maynard opened the door. He'd never taken his hand off the knob.

"Hey, Spenser," Lester said, "I got something you haven't seen before." He put his hands behind his back and brought them back out front. In his right hand was a nickel-plated automatic pistol. It looked like a Beretta. "How's that look to you, Mr. Pro?"

I said, "Lester, if you point that thing at me again, I'll take it away from you and shoot you with it." Then I stomped out. The door closed behind me and I headed for the street.

Outside, the wind was hotter and stronger. I drove home in such a funk that I didn't even check the skirts on the girls, something I did normally as a matter of course, even on still days. Across the street from my apartment was a city car, and in it were Belson and the cop named Billy.

I walked over to the car. "You guys want something or are you hiding from the watch commander?"

"Lieutenant wants you," Billy said.

"Maybe I don't want him."

Belson was slumped down in the passenger seat with his hand over his eyes. He said, "Aw knock off the bullshit, Spenser. Get in the car. Quirk wants you and we both know you're going to come."

He was right, of course. The way I felt if someone said up I'd say down. I got in the back seat. In the two minutes it took us to drive to police headquarters no one said anything.

Quirk's office had moved since last time. He was third-floor front now, facing out onto Berkeley Street. With a view of the secretaries from the insurance companies when they broke for lunch. On his door it said COM-MANDER, HOMICIDE.

Belson knocked and opened the door. "Here he is, Marty."

Quirk sat at a desk that had nothing on it but a phone and a clear plastic cube containing pictures of his family. He was immaculate and impervious, as he had been every other time I ever saw him. I wondered if his bedroom slippers had a spit shine. Probably didn't own bedroom slippers. Probably didn't sleep. He said, "Thanks, Frank. I'll see him alone."

Belson nodded and closed the door behind me. There was a straight chair in front of the desk. I sat in it. Quirk looked at me without saying anything. I looked back. There was a traffic cop outside at the Stuart Street inter-section and I could hear his whistle as he moved cars around the construction.

Quirk said, "I think you burned those two studs up in Saugus."

I said, "Uh-huh."

"I think you set them up and burned them."

"Uh-huh."

"I went up and took a look early this morning. One of the MDC people asked me to.

Informal. Doerr never fired his piece. Wally Hogg did, the magazine's nearly empty, there's a lot of brass up above the death scene in the woods, and there's ricochet marks on one side of the big rock. There's also six spent twelve-gauge shells on the ground on the other side of the rock. The shrubs are torn up around where the M-16 brass was. Like somebody fired off about five rounds of shotgun into the area."

"Uh-huh."

"You knew that Doerr was gunning for you. You let him know you'd be there and you figured they'd try to back-shoot you and you figured you could beat them. And you were right."

"That's really swell, Quirk, you got some swell imagination."

"It's more than imagination, Spenser. You're around buying me a drink, asking about Frank Doerr. Next day I get a tip that Doerr is going to blow you up, and this morning I was looking at Doerr and his gunsel dead up in the woods. You got an alibi for yesterday afternoon and evening?"

"Do I need one?"

Quirk picked up the clear plastic cube on his desk and looked at the pictures of his family. In the outer office a phone rang. A typewriter clacked uncertainly. Quirk put the cube down again on the desk and looked at me.

"No," he said. "I don't think you do."

"You mean you didn't share your theories with the Saugus cops?"

"It's not my territory."

"Then why the hell am I sitting here nodding my head while you talk?"

"Because this is my territory." The hesitant typist in the outer office was still hunting and pecking. "Look, Spenser, I am not in sorrow's clutch because Frank Doerr and his animal went down. And I'm not even all that unhappy that you put them down. There's a lot of guys couldn't do it, and a lot of guys wouldn't try. I don't know why you did it, but I guess probably it wasn't for dough and maybe it wasn't even for protection. If I had to guess, I'd guess it might have been to take the squeeze off of someone else. The squeezee, you might say."

"You might," I said. "I wouldn't."

"Yeah. Anyway. I'm saying to you you didn't burn them in my city. And I'm kind of glad they're burnt. But . . ." Quirk paused and looked at me. His stare was as heavy and solid as his fist. "Don't do it ever in my city."

I said nothing.

"And," he said, "don't start thinking you're some kind of goddamned vigilante. If you get away with this, don't get tempted to do it again. Here or anywhere. You understand what I'm saying to you?"

"Yeah. I do."

"We've known each other awhile, Spenser, and maybe we got a certain amount of respect. But we're not friends. And I'm not a guy you know. I'm a cop."

"Nothing else?"

"Yeah," Quirk said, "something else. I'm a husband and a father and a cop. But the last one's the only thing that makes any difference to you."

"No, not quite. The husband and father makes a difference too. Nobody should be just a job."

"Okay, we agree. But believe what I tell you. I won't bite this bullet again."

"Got it," I said.

"Good."

I stood up, started for the door and stopped, and turned around and said, "Marty?"

"Yeah?"

"Shake," I said.

He put his hand out across his desk, and we did.

28

No one drove me home. It's a short walk from Berkeley Street to my place, and I liked the walk. It gave me time to think, and I needed time. A lot had happened in a short while, and not all of it was going my way. I hadn't thought it would, but there's always hope.

It was afternoon when I got home. I made two lettuce and tomato sandwiches on home-made wheat bread, poured a glass of milk, sat at the counter, and ate and drank the milk and thought about where I was at and where the Rabbs were at and where Bucky Maynard was at. I knew where Doerr and his gunner were at. I had a piece of rhubarb pie for dessert. Put the dishes in the dishwasher, wiped the counter off with a sponge, washed my hands and face, and headed for Church Park.

It was in walking distance and I walked. The wind was still strong, but there was less grit in the air along Marlborough Street, and what little there was rattled harmlessly on my sunglasses. Linda Rabb let me in.

"I heard on the radio that what's'isname Doerr and another man were killed," she said. She wore a loose sleeveless dress, striped black

and white like mattress ticking, and white sandals. Her hair was in two braids, each tied
with a small white ribbon, and her face was
without makeup.

"Yeah, me too," I said. "Your husband
home?"

"No, he's gone to the park."

"Your boy?"

"He's in nursery school."

"We need to talk," I said.

She nodded. "Would you like coffee or anything?"

"Yeah, coffee would be good."

"Instant okay?"

"Sure, black."

I sat in the living room while she made coffee. From the kitchen came the faintly hys-
terical sounds of daytime television. The set
clicked off and Linda Rabb returned, carrying
a round black tray with two cups of coffee
on it. I took one.

"I've talked with Bucky Maynard," I said,
and sipped the coffee. "He won't let go."

"Even though Doerr is dead?" Linda Rabb
was sitting on an ottoman, her coffee on the
floor beside her.

I nodded. "Now he wants his piece."

We were quiet. Linda Rabb sipped at her
coffee, holding the cup in both hands, letting
the steam warm her face. I drank some more

of mine. It was too hot still, but I drank it anyway. The sound of my swallow seemed loud to me.

"We both know, don't we?" Linda Rabb said.

"I think so," I said.

"If I make a public statement about the way I used to be, we'll be free of Maynard, won't we?"

"I think so," I said. "He can still allege that Marty threw some games, but that implicates him too and he goes down the tube with you. I don't think he will. He gets nothing out of it. No money, nothing. And his career is shot as bad as Marty's."

She kept her face buried in the coffee cup.

"I can't think of another way," I said.

She lifted her face and looked at me and said, "Could you kill him?"

I said, "No."

She nodded, without expression. "What would be the best way to confess?"

"I will find you a reporter and you tell the story any way you wish, but leave out the blackmail. That way there's no press conferences, photographers, whatever. After he publishes the story, you refer all inquiry to me. You got any money in the house?"

"Of course."

"Okay, give me a dollar," I said.

She went to the kitchen and returned with a dollar bill. I took out one of my business cards and acknowledged receipt on the back of it and gave it to her.

"Now you are my client," I said. "I represent you."

She nodded again.

"How about Marty?" I said. "Don't you want to clear it with him or discuss it? Or something?"

"No," she said. "You get me the reporter. I'll give him my statement. Then I'll tell Marty. I never bother him before a game. It's one of our rules."

"Okay," I said. "Where's the phone?"

It was in the kitchen. A red wall phone with a long cord. I dialed a number at the *Globe* and talked to a police reporter named Jack Washington that I had gotten to know when I worked for the Suffolk County DA.

"You know the broad who writes that *Feminine Eye* column? The one that had the Nieman Fellowship to Harvard last year?"

"Yeah, she'd love to hear you call her a broad."

"She won't. Can you get her to come to an address I'll give you? If she'll come, she'll get a major news story exclusively. My word, but I can't tell you more than that."

"I can ask her," Washington said. There

was silence and the distant sound of genderless voices. Then a woman's voice said, "Hello, this is Carol Curtis."

I repeated what I'd said to Washington.

"Why me, Mr. Spenser?"

"Because I read your column and you are a class person when you write. This is a story that needs more than who, what, when, and where. It involves a woman and a lot of pain, and more to come, and I don't want some heavy-handed slug with a press pass in his hatband screwing it up."

"I'll come. What's the address?"

I gave it to her and she hung up. So did I.

When I hung up, Linda Rabb asked, "Would you like more coffee? The water's hot."

"Yes, please."

She put a spoonful of instant coffee in my cup, added hot water, and stirred.

"Would you care for a piece of cake or some cookies or anything?"

I shook my head. "No, thanks," I said. "This is fine."

We went back to the living room and sat down as before. Me on the couch, Linda Rabb on the ottoman. We drank our coffee. It was quiet. There was nothing to say. At two fifteen the door buzzer buzzed. Linda Rabb got up and opened the door.

The woman at the door said, "Hello, I'm Carol Curtis."

"Come in, please. I'm Linda Rabb. Would you like coffee?"

"Yes, thank you."

Carol Curtis was small with brown hair cut short and a lively, innocent-looking face. There was a scatter of freckles across her nose and cheekbones, and her light blue eyes were shadowed with long thick lashes. She had on a pink dress with tan figures on it that looked expensive.

Linda Rabb said, "This is Mr. Spenser," and went to the kitchen. I shook hands with Carol Curtis. She had a gold wedding band on her left hand.

"You are the one who called," she said.

"Yeah."

"Jack told me a little about you. It sounded good." She sat on the couch beside me.

"He makes things up," I said.

Linda Rabb came back with coffee and a plate of cookies, which she placed on the coffee table in front of the couch. Then she sat back down on the ottoman and began to speak, looking directly at Carol Curtis as she did.

"My husband is Marty Rabb," she said. "The Red Sox pitcher. But my real name is not Linda, it's Donna, Donna Burlington. Before I married Marty, I was a prostitute in New York and a performer in pornographic films when I met him."

Carol Curtis was saying, "Wait a minute, wait a minute," and rummaging in her purse for pad and pencil. Linda Rabb paused. Carol Curtis got the pad open and wrote rapidly in some kind of shorthand. "When did you meet your husband, Mrs. Rabb?"

"In New York, in what might be called the course of my profession," and off she went. She told it all, in a quiet, uninflected voice the way you might read a story to a child when you'd read it too often. Carol Curtis was a professional. She did not bat one of her thick-lashed eyes after the opening sentence. She asked very little. She understood her subject and she let Linda Rabb talk.

When it was over, she said, "And why are you telling me this?"

Linda Rabb said, "I've lived with it too long. I don't want a secret that will come along and haunt me, later, maybe when my son is older, maybe . . ." She let it hang. Listening, I had the feeling that she had given a real reason. Not the only reason, but a real one.

"Does your husband know?"

"He knows everything."

"Where is he now?"

"At the park."

"Does he know about this . . . ah . . . confession?"

"Yes, he does," Linda said without hesitation.

"And he approves?"

"Absolutely," Linda said.

"Mrs. Rabb," Carol Curtis said. And Linda Rabb shook her head.

"That's all," she said. "I'm sorry. Mr. Spenser represents me and anything else to be said about this he will say." Then she sat still with her hands folded in her lap and looked at me and Carol Curtis sitting on the couch.

I said, "No comment," and Carol Curtis smiled.

"I bet you'll say that often in the future when we talk, won't you?"

"No comment," I said.

"Why is a private detective representing Mrs. Rabb in this? Why not a lawyer or a PR man or perhaps a husband?"

"No comment," I said. And Carol Curtis said it silently along with me, nodding her head as she did so. She closed the notebook and stood up.

"Nice talking with you, Spenser," she said, and put out her hand. We shook. "Don't get up," she said. Then she turned to Linda Rabb.

"Mrs. Rabb," she said and put out her hand.

Linda Rabb took it, and held it for a moment. "You are a saint, Mrs. Rabb. Not a sinner. That's the way I'll write this story."

Linda Rabb said, "Thank you."

"You are also," Carol Curtis said, "a hell of a woman."

29

When Carol Curtis left, I said to Linda Rabb, "Shall I stay with you?"

"I would rather be by myself," she said.

"Okay, but I want to call Harold Erskine and tell him what's coming. I took some of his money and I don't want him blindsided by this. I probably better resign his employ too."

She nodded.

"I'll call him from my office," I said. "Would you like me around when you tell Marty?"

"No," she said. "Thank you."

"I think this will work, kiddo," I said. "If you hear from Maynard, I want to know, right off. Okay?"

"Yes, certainly."

"You know what Carol Curtis said to you?"

She nodded.

"Me too," I said. "Me too."

She smiled at me slightly and didn't move. I let myself out of the apartment and left her sitting on her ottoman. Looking, as far as I could tell, at nothing at all.

I caught a cab to my office and called Harold

Erskine. I told him what Linda Rabb had said in the papers and that it was likely to be on the street in the morning. I told him I'd found not a trace of evidence to suggest that Marty Rabb gambled or threw games or chewed snuff. He was not happy about Linda Rabb, and he was not happy that I didn't know more about it. Or wouldn't tell.

"Goddamnit, Spenser. You are not giving it to me straight. There's more there than you're saying. I hire a man I expect cooperation. You are holding out on me."

I told him I wasn't holding out, and if he thought so, he could refuse to pay my bill. He said he'd think about that too. And we hung up. On my desk were bills and some letters I should get to. I put them in the middle drawer of my desk and closed the drawer. I'd get to them later. Down the street a construction company was tearing down the buildings along the south side of Stuart Street to make room for a medical school. Since early spring they had been moving in on my building. I could hear the big iron wrecking ball thump into the old brick of the garment lofts and palm-reading parlors that used to be there. By next month I'd have to get a new office. What I should do right now is call a real estate broker and get humping on relocation. When you have to move in a hurry, you get screwed.

That's just what I should do. Be smart, move before I had to. I looked at my watch: 4:45. I got up and went out of my office and headed for home. Once I got this cleared up with the Rabbs, I'd look into a new office.

As I walked across the Common, the Hare Krishnas were chanting and hopping around in their ankle-length saffron robes, Hush Puppies and sneakers with white sweat socks poking out beneath the hems. Did you have to look funny to be saved? If Christ were around today, He'd probably be wearing a chambray shirt and flared slacks. There were kids splashing in the wading pool and dogs on leashes and squirrels on the loose and pigeons. In the Public Garden the swan boats were still making their circuit of the duck pond under the little footbridge.

At home I got out a can of beer, read the morning *Globe*, warmed up some leftover beef stew for supper, ate it with Syrian bread while I watched the news, and settled down in my living room with my copy of Morison. I'd bought it in three-volume soft-cover and was halfway through the third volume. I stared at it for half an hour and made no progress at all. I looked at my watch: 7:20. Too early to go to bed. Brenda Loring? No. Susan Silverman? No. Over to the Harbor Health Club and lift a few and talk with Henry Cimoli?

No. Nothing. I didn't want to talk with any-one. And I didn't want to read. I looked at the TV listings in the paper. There was nothing I could stand to look at. And I didn't feel like woodcarving and I didn't feel like sitting in my apartment. If I had a dog, I could take him for a walk. I could pretend.

I went out and strolled along Arlington to Commonwealth and up the mall on Commonwealth toward Kenmore Square. When I got there, I turned down Brookline Ave and went into a bar called Copperfield's and drank beer there till it closed. Then I walked back home and went to bed.

I didn't sleep much, but after a while it was morning and the *Globe* was delivered. There it was, page one, lower left, with a Carol Curtis by-line. SOX WIFE REVEALS OTHER LIFE. I read it, drinking coffee and eating corn bread with strawberry jam, and it was all it should have been. The facts were the way Linda Rabb had given them. The writing was sympathetic and intelligent. Inside on the sports page was a picture of Marty, and one of Linda, obviously taken in the stands on a happier occasion. Balls.

The phone rang. It was Marty Rabb.

"Spenser, the doorman says Maynard and another guy are here to see me. Linda said to call you."

"She there too?"

"Yes."

"I'll be over. Don't let them in until I come."

"Well, shit, I'm not scared . . ."

"Be scared. Lester's got a gun."

I hung up and ran for my car. In less than ten minutes I was in the lobby at Church Park and Bucky and Lester were glaring at me. The houseman called up and we three went together in the same elevator. No one said anything. But the silence in the elevator had the density of clay.

Marty Rabb opened the door and the three of us went in. Me first and Lester last. Linda Rabb came out of the bedroom with her little boy holding on to her hand. Rabb faced us in the middle of the living room. Legs slightly apart, hands on hips. He had on a shortsleeved white shirt, and his lean, wiry arms were tanned halfway up the forearms and pale thereafter. Must pitch with a sweat shirt on, I thought.

"Okay," he said. "Get it done, and then get the hell out of here. All three of you."

Bucky Maynard said, "Ah want to know just what in hell you think you gonna accomplish with that nonsense in the newspapers. You think that's gonna close the account between you and me? 'Cause if you think so, you better think on it some more, boy."

"I thought on it all I'm going to think on it, Maynard," Rabb said. "You and me got nothing else to say to each other."

"You think ah can't squeeze you some more, boy? Ah got records of every game you dumped, boy. Every inning you fudged a run for the office pools, and ah can talk just as good as your little girl to the newspapers, don't you think ah can't."

Lester was leaning bonelessly against the wall by the door with his arms across his chest and his jaws working. He was doing Che Guevara today, starched fatigue pants, engineer boots, a fatigue shirt with the sleeves cut off, and black beret. The shirt hung outside the pants. I wondered if he had the nickel-plated Beretta stuck in his belt.

"You can," I said. "But you won't."

Linda and the boy stood beside Marty, Linda's left hand touching his arm, her right holding the boy's.

"Ah won't?"

"Nope. Because you can't do it without sinking yourself too. You won't make any money by turning him in and you can't do it without getting caught yourself. Marty will be out of the league, okay. But so will you, fats."

Maynard's face got bright red. "You think so?" he said.

"Yeah. You say one word to anybody and you'll be calling drag races in Dalrymple, Georgia. And you know it."

Everybody looked at everybody. No one said anything. Lester cracked his gum. Then Rabb said, "So it looks like I got you and you got me. That's a tie, you fat bastard. And that's the way it'll end. But I tell you one time: I'll pitch and you broadcast, but you come near me or my wife or my kid and I will kill you."

Lester said, "You can't kill shit."

Rabb kept looking at Maynard. "And keep that goddamn freak away from me," he said, "or I'll kill him too."

Lester moved away from the wall, the slouch gone. He shrugged into his tae kwon do stance like a man putting on armor.

The little boy said, "Momma," not very loud, but with tears in it.

Marty said, "Get him out of here, Linda." And the woman and the boy backed away toward the bedroom. Maynard's face was red and sweaty.

"Hey, kid," Lester said, "your momma's a whore."

Rabb swung a looping left hand that Lester shucked off his forearm. He planted his left foot and swung his right around in a complete circle so that the back of his heel caught Rabb in the right side, at the kidneys. The kick had turned Lester all the way around. But he spun back forward like an unwinding spring. He was good. The kick staggered Rabb but didn't put him down. The next one would, and if it didn't, Lester would really hurt him. Maybe he already had. A kick like that will rupture a kidney.

Linda Rabb said, "Spenser." And grabbed hold of her husband, both arms around him. "Stop it, Marty," she said, "stop it." The boy pressed against her leg and his father's. Marty Rabb dragged his wife and son with him as he started back toward Lester. Lester was back in his stance, blowing a big bubble and chewing it back in again. He was about three feet to my left. I took one step and sucker-punched him in the neck, behind the ear. He fell down, his legs folding under him at the knees so that he sank to the floor like a penitent in prayer.

"Marty," I said, "get your wife and kid out of here. You don't want the kid seeing this. Look at him."

The kid was in a huddle of terror against his mother's leg. Marty reached down and picked him up, and with his other arm tight around Linda Rabb, he hustled them into the bedroom.

"I will say to you what Rabb did, you great

sack of guts," I said. "You and your clothes-horse stay away from Rabb as long as you live or I will put you both in the hospital."

Lester came off the floor at me, but he was wobbly. He tried the kick again, but it was too slow. I leaned away from it. I moved in behind the kick and drove a left at his stomach. He blocked it and hit me in the solar plexus. I tensed for it, but it still made me numb. A good punch turning the fist over as it came, but there wasn't as much steam as there should have been behind it, and I was inside now, up against him. I had weight on him, maybe fifteen pounds, and I was stronger. As long as I stayed up against him, I could neutralize his quickness and I could outmuscle him. I rammed him against the wall. My chin was locked over his shoulder, and I hit him in the stomach with both fists. I hurt him. He grunted. He hammered on my back with both fists, but I had a lot of muscle layer to protect back there. Twenty years of working on the lats and the lateral obliques. I got hold of his shirtfront with both hands and pulled him away from the wall and slammed him back up against it. His hand whiplashed back and banged on the wall. It was plasterboard and it broke through. I slammed him again and he sagged. I brought my left fist up over his arms and hit him on the side of the face, at the temple, with the side of my clenched fist. Don't want to break the knuckles. A kind of pressure was building in me, and I saw everything indistinctly. I slammed him on the wall and then stepped back and hit him left, left, right, in the face. I could barely see his face now, white and disembodied in front of me. I hit it again. He started to sag, I got hold of his collar with my left hand and pulled him up and hit him with my right. He sagged heavier, and I jammed him against the wall with my left and hammered him with my right. His face was no longer white. It was bloody, and it bobbled limply when I hit him. I could feel my whole self surging up into my fist as I held him and hit him. The rhythm of the punches thundered in my head, and I couldn't hear anything else. I was vaguely aware of someone pulling at me and I brushed him away with my right hand. Then I could hear voices. I kept punching. Then I could hear Linda Rabb's voice. The pounding in my head modified a little.

"Stop it, Spenser. Stop it, Spenser. You're killing him. Stop it."

Someone had hold of my arm, and it was Marty Rabb, and Lester's face was a bloody mess, unconscious in front of me. Maynard was sitting openmouthed on the floor, blood trickling from his nose. It must have been him

I brushed away.

"Stop it, stop it, stop it." Linda Rabb had hold of my left arm and was trying to pry my hand loose from Lester's shirtfront. I opened the fingers and stepped away, and Lester slid to the floor. Maynard slid over to him without getting up and with a handkerchief began to wipe the blood from Lester's face. I could see Lester's chest rising and falling as he breathed. I noticed I was breathing heavy too. Marty and Linda Rabb both stood in front of me, the kid holding Linda's hand. Tears were running down his cheeks and his eyes were wide with fright, but he was quiet.

"Jesus, Spenser," Rabb said. "What happened? You were crazy."

I was sweating now, as if a fever had broken. I shook my head. "A lot of strain," I said. "We've all had a lot of strain. I'm sorry the kid saw it."

Maynard had gone to the bathroom and come back with wet towels and was cleaning Lester up and putting a cold compress on his forehead. "Pay attention to what happened, Bucky boy," I said. "Don't irritate me."

Lester moved a little. His lips were swollen and one eye was closed. Maynard kept washing his face with the damp towel.

"It's okay, Lester," he said. "It's okay."

273

Lester sat up and pushed the towel away. "Help me up," he mumbled.

Maynard got up and got Lester on his feet. "Let's get out of here," Lester said.

Maynard started to take him toward the door, his arm around Lester's back.

"Bucky," I said, "we agree about the tie? And how we got no further business?"

Maynard nodded. There was no color left in his face, just the slight smear of brown, drying blood on his lip.

"I want to go home, Bucky," Lester mumbled, and Bucky said, "Yeah, yeah, Lester, we'll go home." And out they went.

Linda Rabb sat on the floor with her son and held him against her and put her face in his hair. They rocked back and forth slightly on the floor, and Marty Rabb and I stood awkwardly above them and said nothing at all. Finally I said, "Okay, Marty. I think we've done all there is to do."

He put his hand out. "Thank you, Spenser, I guess. We were in a mess we couldn't have gotten out of without you. I can't say quite where we're at now, but thank you for what you did. Including Lester. I think probably he's too good at tae kwon dong or whatever it is for me."

"He might have been too good for me if I hadn't sucker-punched him first."

We shook hands. Linda Rabb didn't look up. I went out the front door. She didn't say goodbye.

I never saw her again.

30

"And you kept hitting him," Susan Silverman said.

We were sitting in a back booth in The Last Hurrah, looking at the menu and having the first drink of the evening. Mine was a stein of Harp; hers, a vodka gimlet.

"It all seemed to bubble up inside me and explode. It wasn't Lester; it was Doerr and Wally Hogg and me and the case and the way things worked out so everyone got hurt some. It all just exploded out of me, and I damn near killed the poor creep."

"From what you say he probably earned the beating."

"Yeah, he did. That's not what bothers me. I'm what bothers me. I'm not supposed to do that."

"I know, I've seen the big red *S* on your chest."

"That ain't all you seen, sweet patooti."

"I know, but it's all I remember."

"Oh," I said.

She smiled at me, that sunrise of a smile that colored her whole face and seemed to enliven her whole body. "Well, maybe I can remember something else if I think on it."

"Perhaps a refresher course later on tonight," I said.

"Perhaps."

The waiter came and took our order, went away, and returned shortly with another beer for me.

"The irony is," I said, "that Linda Rabb is married to one of the all-time greats of jockdom, and she's being helped by me, with the red *S* on my chest and the gun in my pocket, and she's the one that saves them. She's the one, while us two stud ducks are standing around flexing, that does what had to be done. And it hurt and I couldn't save them and her husband couldn't save them. She saved herself and her husband."

"Maynard has stopped the blackmail?"

"Sure, he had to. He had nothing to gain and everything to lose." I drank some beer. The waiter brought us each a plate of oysters and a bottle of Chablis.

"The papers have been kind to Mrs. Rabb."

"Yeah, pretty good. There's been a lot of mail, some of it really ugly, but the club publicity people are handling it and she hasn't had to read much of it."

"How about Marty?"

"He went into the stands for some guy out in Minnesota and got a three-day suspension for it. Since then he's kept his mouth shut, but you can tell it hurts."

"And you?"

I shrugged. The waiter took away the empty oyster plates and put down two small crocks of crab and lobster stew.

"And you?" she said again.

"I killed two guys, and almost killed another one."

"Killing those two was what made it possible for Linda Rabb to do what she did."

"I know."

"You've killed people before."

"Yeah."

"They would have killed you."

"Yeah."

"Then it had to be, didn't it?"

"I set them up," I said. "I got them up there to kill them."

"Yes, and you walked in on them from the front, two of them to one of you, like a John Wayne movie. How many men do you think would have done that?"

I shook my head.

"Do you think they would have done it? They weren't doing it. They were trying to ambush you. And if they'd succeeded, would they be agonizing about it now?"

I shook my head again.

"You'd have had to kill them," Susan said.

"Sometime. Now it's done. What does it matter how?"

"That's the part that does matter. How. It's the only part that matters."

"Honor?" Susan said.

"Yeah," I said. The waiter came and took the crocks and returned with scrod for Susan and steak for me. We ate a little.

"I am not making fun," Susan said, "but aren't you older and wiser than that?"

I shook my head. "Nope. Neither is Rabb. I know what's killing him. It's killing me too. The code didn't work."

"The code," Susan said.

"Yeah, jock ethic, honor, code, whatever. It didn't cover this situation."

"Can't it be adjusted?"

"Then it's not a code anymore. See, being a person is kind of random and arbitrary business. You may have noticed that. And you need to believe in something to keep it from being too random and arbitrary to handle. Some people take religion, or success, or patriotism, or family, but for a lot of guys those things don't work. A guy like me. I don't have religion or family, that sort of thing. So you accept some system of order, and you stick to it. For Rabb it's playing ball. You give it all you got and you play hurt and you don't complain and so on and if you're good you win and the better you are the more you win so the more you win the more you prove you're good. But for Rabb it's also taking care of the wife and kid, and the two systems came into conflict. He couldn't be true to both. And now he's compromised and he'll never have the same sense of self he had before."

"And you, Spenser?"

"Me too, I guess. I don't know if there is even a name for the system I've chosen, but it has to do with honor. And honor is behavior for its own reason. You know?"

"Who has it," Susan said, "he that died a Wednesday?"

"Yeah, sure, I know that too. But all I have is how I act. It's the only system I fit into. Whatever the hell I am is based in part on not doing things I don't think I should do. Or don't want to do. That's why I couldn't last with the cops. That's the difference between me and Martin Quirk."

"Perhaps Quirk has simply chosen a different system," Susan said.

"Yeah. I think he has. You're catching on."

"And," Susan said, "two moral imperatives in your system are never to allow innocents to be victimized and never to kill people except involuntarily. Perhaps the words aren't quite the right ones, but that's the idea, isn't it?"

I nodded.

"And," she said, "this time you couldn't obey both those imperatives. You had to violate one."

I nodded again.

"I understand," she said.

We ate for a bit in silence.

"I can't make it better," she said.

"No," I said. "You can't."

We ate the rest of the entrée in silence.

The waiter brought coffee. "You will live a little diminished, won't you?" she said.

"Well, I got a small sniff of my own mortality. I guess everyone does once in a while. I don't know if that's diminishment or not. Maybe it's got to do with being human."

She looked at me over her coffee cup. "I think maybe it has to do with that," she said.

I didn't feel good, but I felt better. The waiter brought the check.

Outside on Tremont Street, Susan put her arm through mine. It was a warm night and there were stars out. We walked down toward the Common.

"Spenser," she said, "you are a classic case for the feminist movement. A captive of the male mystique, and all that. And I want to say, for God's sake, you fool, outgrow all that Hemingwayesque nonsense. And yet . . ." She leaned her head against my shoulder as she spoke. "And yet I'm not sure you're wrong.

I'm not sure but what you are exactly what you ought to be. What I am sure of is I'd care for you less if killing those people didn't bother you."

At Park Street we crossed to the Common and walked down the long walk toward the Public Garden. The swan boats were docked for the night. We crossed Arlington onto Marlborough Street and turned in at my apartment. We went up in silence. Her arm still through mine. I opened the door and she went in ahead of me. Inside the door, with the lights still out, I put my arms around her and said, "Suze, I think I can work you into my system."

"Enough with the love talk," she said. "Off with the clothes."

The employees of THORNDIKE PRESS hope you have enjoyed this Large Print book. All our Large Print titles are designed for easy reading, and all our books are made to last. Other Thorndike Large Print books are available at your library, through selected bookstores, or directly from us. For more information about current and upcoming titles, please call or mail your name and address to:

THORNDIKE PRESS
PO Box 159
Thorndike, Maine 04986
800/223-6121
207/948-2962